# SHATTERED TRUST

MONROE FAMILY

CHRISTIAN ROMANCE

LAURA SCOTT

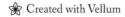 Created with Vellum

# PROLOGUE

"Head for the river! *Run!*"

Austin Monroe could barely hear Sam's voice over the roar of the wildfire bearing down on them. He didn't need his buddy's urging to keep him moving—the heat of the fire scorching his back was motivation enough. The wind had shifted, bringing the fire they'd been fighting straight toward them, breaking through the line. If not for Sam coming back to warn him, he would have been burned to a crisp.

They still might die.

Even as the realization sink deep, he caught sight of the river less than fifty yards ahead. Reaching the river before the fire caught up to them was their only chance of survival.

A slim chance, if the severe drought hadn't made the river too low.

The heavy Kevlar suit he wore wasn't enough to keep the force of the heat off him. He ignored the sweat rolling into his eyes beneath the helmet as he stayed focused on the river. He slipped, nearly fell, but Sam was right behind him, dragging him upright and pushing him forward. With a herculean effort, he made his way down the bank to the water, jumping in with a feeling of relief. He doused his whole body as best he could in water that was barely knee high.

It took him a minute to realize Sam hadn't joined him in the river. He glanced back to see his partner using a drip torch to light a backfire on the grassy area surrounding the riverbank to protect them from a lethal burn over.

He pulled himself back out of the water to join Sam. They didn't have much time as the wildfire bore down on them, moving with astronomical speed as it gobbled up the dry brush with a voracious hunger.

"Get into the river!" Sam shouted as he lit as many fires as he could with the drip torch. Austin had lost his equipment when the fire had changed direction, so he couldn't do much to help.

"No." He wasn't leaving his partner, the guy who'd come back for him. He would not allow Sam to face this alone. When the drip torch was empty, Sam tossed it into the smoldering grass fire. Austin grabbed his arm. "Let's go. We need to get in the water."

This time Sam didn't argue, but finally followed him back down the bank to the river. When Austin hit the water, he felt Sam fall heavily unto him from behind, pinning him down. It seemed as if his buddy had used up all his resources to keep going. Austin reached up and pulled Sam down into the water beside him.

The backfire didn't work as well as they'd hoped. Orange flames flickered dangerously close. Following Sam's lead, Austin took a big gulp of air before submerging his head in the river leaving only the very top of his helmet above the water. He sensed Sam did the same, although the smoke was so thick it was hard to see.

Over and over again, he quickly lifted his head, gasped

for what little oxygen was left in the air and then ducked his head beneath the water again.

Finally the roar of the fire subsided, indicating it had burned down, the raging beast having moved on to better prey—thick brush lining the ridge to the west of them.

"Sam?" He levered himself to his hands and knees, reaching for his friend. Sam's smoke blackened face peered up at him and his heart squeezed in his chest. Hadn't Sam continued dunking his head beneath the water? "Are you all right?"

Sam gave a tiny nod, but his breathing was harsh, labored. Austin reached for his radio, wondering just how much smoke had gotten into his buddy's lungs. "Mayday, mayday. Firefighter with smoke inhalation is down in the Rock River, two miles east of the river's bend. Need medic STAT."

"Roger that. Medevac chopper on the way."

"Sam?" Panic clawed up his back as Sam began to cough, his body convulsing so hard he could barely take a breath. "Hang on, they're coming for us. Just hang on."

"Lindsey." Sam reached up and weakly grasped Austin's jacket. "Take care of her. Take care of Lindsey and Josh."

Sam's plea for his wife and child stabbed his heart. His gut clenched with fear. "Don't worry about Lindsey and Josh. You're going to make it out of here to care for them yourself."

"Too late," Sam whispered between coughing fits. "Take care of them—promise me. They'll need... Promise me..." His voice faded as another coughing fit seized him.

"I promise." Austin held his partner close, scanning the smoke darkened sky. Where in the world was that chopper?

Sam stopped coughing, closed his eyes and slumped

bonelessly in Austin's arms. No. No! He stared down at his buddy's face, as the medivac chopper cleared the trees and headed for them, knowing with a sick certainty that Sam was right.

It was too late.

# CHAPTER ONE

Smoke. Accompanied by the wail of sirens.

Lindsey Winters was used to sirens—they blared past her house often in this part of the city—but it was the acrid smell of smoke that forced her to climb out of her sofa bed located in the center of the living room.

A quick glance around showed nothing amiss. The living room and kitchen were essentially one room, and she hadn't left a candle burning. There wasn't any other obvious source of smoke. One thing about having a small house was that there weren't too many places to look for a fire.

She hastily pulled on a robe and headed down the hall to the single bedroom toward the back of the cottage, where her nine-year-old son slept. "Josh?"

"Mom?" He answered in a sleepy tone, having just woken up. "Do you smell smoke? I thought I was dreaming about Dad."

"It's not a dream, Josh." Her heart squeezed for her son, who obviously missed his father. Sam had died six months ago, and so much had happened since then, not least of all the recent move to this house. She could understand why he'd make the connection. When her firefighter husband had been alive, he'd often come home reeking of smoke. The kind that came from fighting fires, not from smoking cigarettes or cigars.

It was the same cent filling the air now. "Come here." She gathered him in a one armed hug. "Let's see what's going on."

In the living room, red and blue lights flashed brightly through the front window. Screaming fire trucks pulled up, blocking the end of their driveway. Pressing her nose against the glass, she peered out and saw firefighters and police gathering around the house next door. It was the Tolliver's place. They're hadn't been time to get to know her neighbors, but she had briefly met single mom Anna Tolliver and her two girls, who were both a few years younger than Josh.

"Wow," Josh whispered beside her. Now that he realized their house wasn't the one on fire, he relaxed a little. "I've never seen a fire this close."

"Me neither," she admitted. As a nurse working in the emergency department of a small Community Hospital, she'd been exposed to the occasional burn patient, but nothing very serious. The really bad burn cases were airlifted to Los Angeles.

She shivered, despite the warmth of the balmy California spring night.

A firefighter dressed in full gear jogged across her front lawn, straight toward her front door. She pulled back in surprise, and then went over to open the door before he had a chance to knock.

"Lindsey?" Her husband's best friend and fellow firefighter and paramedic, Austin Monroe gaped at her in shock. "What on earth are you doing here?"

Great. Just what she needed. Not. She stifled a sigh and

angled her chin, fervently wishing that out of all the fire-fighters in Sun Valley, Austin Monroe hadn't been on duty tonight. "We live here."

"What? Since when? "Then he gave an impatient shake of his head. "Never mind. Come on, we need you and Josh to evacuate the premises. The fire next door is too close and too far out of control to ensure your safety.

"Is there time for us to change our clothes?" She rubbed one bare foot over the other.

He frowned, glancing down at her bare toes, and then at her sons equally bare feet. "Two minutes. If you're not ready by then, I'm coming in after you."

No need for threats—she believed him. Turning away from the door, she gave Josh a slight push. "Get dressed. Hurry." As he disappeared down the hall, she grabbed the closest pair of jeans, sweater, socks and comfortable running shoes she could find before ducking into the bathroom to change.

In less than two minutes she met Josh and headed outside, resisting the urge to gather her meager yet precious belongings. Through the mass of people milling about she saw Anna Tolliver and her girls standing off to the side, surrounded by police. Thank heavens they were safe.

Austin nodded with approval when they stepped out onto the front porch. He directed them to a spot safely beyond the perimeter of the fire. "I need both of you to stand back here, out of the way."

Again, she wasn't going to argue. Austin had been her husband's smoke jumping partner and he knew his way around fires, whether they were domestic like at the Tolliver 's house or a thick, raging wildfire. Smoke jumpers were men who fought wildfires by jumping from planes into smoke filled skies to help prevent the fire from spreading.

Her husband and Austin had both trained as smoke jumpers. She hadn't understood the attraction, something she and Sam had fought about.

Now she was grateful for Austin's experience in fighting fires.

From their safety zone Lindsey could see orange flames dancing through the kitchen window of the Tolliver's house. She swallowed hard when she realized how close the threat was to her home. Flames reached up, like gnarled fingers trying to grasp the edge of her roof. The postage-stamp sized lots on which their small bungalow homes were built only gave a couple of feet of clearance between them.

"Lindsey?" Austin lightly grasped her arm.

She tore her gaze from the horrifying image of the flames leaping toward her home. "What?"

"Don't leave without me, okay?" His intense gaze searched hers. "I'll take care of you and Josh. Just wait for me."

Her throat was clogged with fear so she simply nodded. No matter how annoyed she had been with him earlier, it was nice to know she wasn't totally alone in the world. Austin may be a bit of an interfering control freak, but he was definitely a man of his word. Her gaze followed him as he turned and jogged back, taking his role in fighting the fire. She intended to watch him work, but quickly lost him amidst the sea of firefighters, unable to distinguish him from the others beneath their heavy gear.

"Mom?" Josh asked in a tiny, scared voice. "Is our house going to burn, too?"

She clutched him close, wishing she could sound positive when she had a sinking feeling their situation was about to go from bad to worse. After Sam had died, she'd discovered a mountain of debt. Likely the reason he'd taken the smoke jumping jobs. Not that it had changed the inevitable outcome. She'd been forced to sell the house, grasping the first meager offer that had come in, and had moved here into this tiny one bedroom home in a not so nice part of town.

This probably wasn't the time to admit she had absolutely no insurance. They'd only moved in two months ago, and her loan had been low enough that the bank hadn't forced the issue. It had been difficult enough to make sure there had been money for food and gas, much less for homeowners' insurance.

Now she realized how foolish she'd been. "I hope not, Josh." She watched the flames of her neighbor's house dance closer. The firefighters aimed a wide, forceful stream of water directly toward the source of the fire, completely drenching her house in the process.

She should be glad that no one was hurt, but what would happen if their house did catch fire? Where would they go? Where would they live?

She blinked away tears of useless self-pity. "I really hope not," she whispered.

---

REELING from the shock of finding Lindsey and Josh in the tiny, cramped house on Puckett Street, Austin concentrated on fighting the fire. Thankfully the occupants of the home had gotten out safely, but the fire, having somehow started in the electrical system inside the walls, had traveled along the electrical wires, engulfing the entire place before anyone had understood what had happened.

The house was a total loss. The goal now was to contain the fire, preventing it from spreading to the homes on either side.

Particularly to Lindsey's house.

He didn't understand what had happened. Why had she moved out of the nice place she'd lived in with Sam? Because of the memories? Or for financial reasons? As much as he tried to be there for Lindsey, especially during those first few weeks after Sam's death, she'd resisted his support. They'd had a huge fight when he tried to give her some advice on how to handle Josh. She'd shouted at him to get a life of his own and to leave her alone.

He'd backed off, giving her the space she'd asked for. He hadn't been to see her in four months. First, he'd headed off to a three week smoke jumping tour, having been dropped via parachute into the depths of the Oregon forest, and then when he'd gotten back he'd gone home to visit his parents. He'd been haunted by memories of Sam the whole time he had been in Oregon. And at his parent's home, too.

He often saw his buddy's smoke covered face in his dreams. His nightmares.

And he'd failed Sam again, because things were obviously worse for Lindsey than he'd realized. She'd kicked him out of her life once, but he shouldn't have left so easily. He'd assumed she'd at least been happily settled in her home. He never wanted to hurt her, but this time he wasn't leaving until he knew she and Josh were safe and secure.

Preferably not living in that death trap masquerading as a house.

When they finally had the fire under control, he helped stow the gear, his gaze searching for Lindsey and Josh. He figured the police had gotten the Red Cross involved to help locate the family that had just lost their home. There was no way he would allow Lindsey and Josh to return to their place either, not until he'd had the structure thoroughly checked out.

Might be a good idea to check the electrical wiring in the place, too. He had a sneaking suspicion it wasn't up to code, as the footprint of Lindsey's house was exactly the same as the one that had gone up in flames. Just the thought of faulty wiring lining the walls of her home made his blood run cold.

"Lindsey?" He made his way over to where she and Josh both stood, looking shell shocked, their arms wrapped around each other for support. "I'll take you over to my place for what's left of the night."

She frowned. "Why can't we go back to our house?"

"I'm sorry, there's been water and smoke damage. He was glad he didn't have to lie—there had been a lot of water damage. "I'm afraid the house needs to be cleared by us before you can move back in."

"Oh." She bit her lip and shrugged. "Well, then, a hotel is fine. We don't need to impose on you."

"You're not imposing." Just once he wished she'd simply give in and let him help. Although she didn't realize how much his need to offer her assistance was wrapped in guilt over being the cause of Sam's death. "Actually, it may be better if you drove your car so you're not stranded without a set of wheels."

She seemed to like that idea, but still hesitated, her gaze uncertain. "I don't know—a hotel might be better if this is going to take a while."

"A few days at the most," he said even though he didn't point out that if the house needed repairs, the time frame would be undoubtedly longer. "Please? At least for tonight?"

She grudgingly nodded. "Can we pack some of our things?"

"Yes." He was grateful to give her at least that much.

His crew was standing around, waiting for him, but he waved them off, figuring he'd get a ride back to the fire station later and followed her inside.

The place was even smaller than he'd realized. Frowning at the open, rumpled sofa sleeper taking up most of the living room, he watched as she gathered clothing together, throwing them into an old, well-worn suitcase.

He didn't like the circumstances she was living in, that's for sure. She didn't even have a bedroom of her own. Once again, he wondered what had happened? What had caused her to move from the nice three-bedroom house she lived in with Sam to this? What's more, why had she moved without even telling him?

Or had she deliberately moved just to avoid him?

No, that didn't make sense. He'd honored her wishes, leaving her alone.

Lindsey closed the suitcase and bent over to pick it up.

"I'll take that." He stepped forward to lift the heavy case from her grasp. He lugged the suitcase outside and put it in the trunk of Lindsey's bright yellow car. Lindsey loved the color yellow, and seeing her small car would normally make him smile. But not tonight. Upon returning inside, he went back to find Lindsey and Josh in the single bedroom located at the rear of the house. Josh's suitcase was full, so Austin took it before Lindsey could.

"Anything else?" He paused in the doorway, looking at them expectantly.

"I guess not." She gave one last glance around the compact kitchen and living room with a forlorn gaze.

"Hey, don't worry, you'll be back soon." He placed a hand in the small of her back and gently urged her toward the door. "We need to hit the road. You need some sleep. I have two spare bedrooms, one for each of you." She'd only been to his place once so she might not know how many bedrooms he had. She and Josh would be far better off in his place than staying in the tiny house, even if the place was safe to move back into. At least they'd each have their own bedroom.

"Thank heaven's tomorrow is Sunday," Lindsey said with a wide yawn. "Josh will be able to rest before he heads back to school."

"Do you have to work tomorrow?" Lindsey was an emergency department nurse for the Sun Valley Community Hospital, and he'd sometimes run into her when he'd brought patients in from his paramedic runs.

"No." She shook her head. "Not until Monday."

He was glad she'd have a day to recuperate. He was tempted to take over the task of driving but knew she would be irritated if he tried to take control, so he forced himself to hand her car keys over. She raised a brow, a smile tugging at the corner of her mouth, as if she knew what the small gesture had cost him. With this sigh he took off his bulky jacket and hat so he could slide into the passenger seat.

"You and Josh can stay with me as long as necessary," he said in a low tone as she drove to his place, located not too far from the home she's shared with Sam.

"Thanks, but one night should be enough." She barely glanced at him, her attention on the road. He didn't contradict her, hoping he could convince her to stay if her house needed repairs. At least for a while.

She fell silent, so he contented himself with watching her. She was beautiful, even with her long blonde hair mussed and not a speck of makeup on her face. He had a hard time tearing his gaze from her profile. *Knock it off*, he warned himself. This wasn't the time to think about Lindsey as a pretty woman he was attracted to. He'd promised Sam he'd take care of them. Lindsey needed a friend. A helping hand. A shoulder to lean on.

Not a man who fantasized about something more.

A fresh wave of guilt hit low in his belly. First, he'd caused his partner's death, robbing Lindsey and Josh of a husband and father. Then he'd botched his attempt to help her. What was wrong with him that he was attracted to his best friend's widow?

Could he sink any lower?

He'd had girlfriends in the past, but nothing serious. He'd preferred being foot-loose and fancy free. He came from a large family with brothers and sisters and parents who had been married for over forty years. If he was to marry, he wanted a relationship like his parents. But since he hadn't found anyone that remotely interested him, he'd decided he wasn't the type to settle down.

So why was he so interested in the one woman who had marriage and family written all over her? A woman with a nine-year-old son who needed a father?

He gave himself a mental shake. He'd always admired Lindsey from afar, but she was strictly off limits.

The sooner his hormones figured that out, the better off he would be.

# CHAPTER TWO

When Lindsey awoke, the sun streaming in through the window was on the wrong side of the room. She blinked, disoriented by her strange surroundings, and then gradually realized where she was.

Austin's house. She and Josh were sleeping in the two spare bedrooms of Austin's home after their neighbor's horrible house fire. Thankfully no one had been hurt.

The tantalizing aroma of bacon and eggs made her stomach growl, reminding her it had been way too many hours since her last meal.

If you could even call macaroni and cheese out of a box, a meal.

Scrambling from the wide bed, she headed for the shower. Sleeping in a regular bed rather than a sofa sleeper had her feeling more rested than ever. She hastily dressed and then took a few minutes to blow dry her hair. Not because she was vain and wanted to look nice for Austin, she told herself. But because she wanted to be ready so she could do whatever needed to be done to obtain permission to move back into her home.

When she emerged from her bedroom, feeling wide awake and ready to face the day, she noticed the door of Josh's room was ajar and her son was nowhere in sight.

He was probably already in the kitchen helping himself to Austin's breakfast. Good thing her son had always gotten along with Austin. The poor kid had been through enough trauma lately, between his problems at school and the recent move away from his friends.

If she had her way, they wouldn't impose on Austin's hospitality for long.

She entered the kitchen trying not to feel self-conscious. "Good morning."

"Hi." Austin's warm and appreciative gaze swept over her. Her mouth went dry as she stared at him. He stood in front of the stove, wearing a fitted paramedic a blue T-shirt that emphasized his broad shoulders and a pair of well-worn jeans that rode low on his hips. His mahogany-colored hair was long and a bit shaggy. Holding a spatula in his hand didn't come close to compromising his masculinity.

*Liar.* Who was she trying to kid? This was the reason she had taken time with her appearance. What was wrong with her? Why couldn't she control this ridiculous attraction to Austin Monroe? Taking a deep breath, she glanced to where Josh was seated at the table, his mouth full of crunchy bacon. She kept her tone light. "Austin, you didn't have to cook for us. I'm sure we could have gotten by with cereal."

He shrugged, dividing his attention between her and the eggs in the frying pan. "I cooked for myself but made enough for everyone. If you're hungry, have a seat."

She was famished, so she pulled up a chair across from Josh and sat down. Less than a minute later, Austin set a plate in front of her with two eggs cooked over easy, wheat toast and two slices of bacon.

Everything made exactly the way she liked it.

His thoughtfulness made her throat close and for a moment she couldn't speak. This was why she'd avoided Austin in the months since Sam's death. Being this close to him was painful because every moment with him only magnified Sam's shortcomings as a husband. He and Sam may have been close friends, but they couldn't have been more different.

"Thanks," she murmured, avoiding his gaze and turning her attention to her food. When he took a seat beside her, she was all too aware of his presence.

The cozy atmosphere in the kitchen was almost too much to bear. She couldn't remember the last time Sam had joined her and Josh for a family meal. For too long Sam had insisted on sitting in front of the television to eat, claiming he needed to relax after his long day at work. They'd grown so far apart over the years since Josh's birth, she sometimes had looked at him and wondered how she'd fallen out of love with him so quickly.

Or if she ever really loved Sam the way he deserved to be loved at all?

She slammed a door on the excruciating memories.

"Do you need to head back to the fire station?" She glanced at Austin. She knew from Sam's schedule, the fire-fighter paramedic crew were usually scheduled for twenty-four hours on duty, then off for forty-eight, unless they were needed for additional shifts.

"Nope, I'm off duty as of this morning."

"Did you get much sleep?" She had driven him back to the fire station last night after he'd brought their suitcases in and had gotten them settled. It had been late before she'd tumbled into bed, close to two in the morning. He must have gotten even less sleep than she had.

"Enough." He shrugged again offering a crooked smile. "I'm used to interrupted sleep with my schedule. It's hard to sleep after the adrenaline rush of fighting fires. Although I have to admit, it was more difficult than usual last night, knowing you'd moved into a house on Puckett Street without telling me."

She focused her attention on her food, wishing she could think of a way to avoid this conversation. "I mailed a change of address note. And there's nothing wrong with living on Puckett Street."

"Yes, there is. None of my friends live there," Josh argued.

Lindsey stifled a sigh. She and Josh had been over this too many times to count. "I'm sure you'll make new friends. And I've been driving you over to your friend's house as often as I can."

Austin frowned. "I didn't get a note."

He hadn't? She frowned, knowing she'd sent one. "Must have gotten lost in the mail." She tried to change the subject. "Do you know what caused the Tolliver's fire?"

"Faulty electrical wiring." He finished his meal in record time, the same way Sam always had. Must be part of the firefighter's strategy—to eat quick before the next call. He held her gaze. "Your house has the same footprint and likely built by the same company, so I'd like to have a professional check out the wiring before you move back in. Especially now, with the potential water damage, too. We drenched your house pretty good to prevent the fire from spreading."

Her heart sank. What he said made sense, but she didn't want to be dependent on him. Hadn't she become too dependent on him the last time he tried to help? Staying with Austin was dangerous to her emotional well-being. Being independent was important to her, now more than ever. "Can you get someone out there first thing Monday morning? I'm working day shift tomorrow."

Austin slowly nodded. "I'll see what I can do."

It was on the tip of her tongue to suggest she could make her own arrangements, but then realized she had no idea where to start. How many electricians did she know? None. Obviously, she would be stupid to refuse Austin's expertise.

At least for this. But if he tried to take over other aspects of her life, she'd have no choice but to leave.

"Can I be excused?" Josh pushed away from the table. "Tony and I want to go skateboarding. He's glad I'm back in the neighborhood."

Austin opened his mouth as if to respond, but then closed it again when she raised a brow in his direction. She turned to her son. "Sure. Be back home by dinner time though."

"Thanks, Mom." Josh disappeared from the kitchen.

"I appreciate you not interfering," she said to Austin, admiring his restraint.

"You're welcome." He hesitated then added, "Lindsey, I know the last time we saw each other, you were very angry with me. I'm sorry if you felt I tried to take over your life. I never meant to hurt you in any way. I care about you and Josh—you're Sam's family for heaven's sake. You must know I only want to help. Please, make yourself at home here, okay?"

He was being too nice. Again. She tried not to feel guilty as he threw her words back at her. She had told him to stop interfering in her life and to leave her alone. During those first few weeks, right after Sam's death, Austin had been glued to her side. In the early days, she'd appreciated his strength and compassion, but after a while, when he'd continued to make decisions for her, especially related to Josh, she'd gotten annoyed. The fact that he was so attractive didn't help.

If she were honest, she'd admit that she'd pushed Austin away for two reasons, her attraction to him and because he had been trying to take over her life. Both were equally dangerous. She needed to remain strong enough to resist him. "I know you're only trying to help. But I need you to understand how important it is to me that I stand on my own two feet."

"Is that why you sold Sam's house?"

"No." She stood and cleared the breakfast dishes from the table. "You cooked, so it's only fair I clean up."

He caught her arm. "Did you sell the house because you couldn't afford it?"

"What difference does it make?" She subtly tried to tug her arm from his grip.

"It makes a lot of difference. I could have given you the money to make your house payments until you received the company life insurance payment."

"I don't want your money, Austin." She jerked out of his grasp. What part of being independent didn't he understand? She wasn't like her mother. She didn't need a man to survive. She could manage just fine on her own. "My financial situation isn't any of your concern. Let's leave it at that, okay?" She turned and busied herself with washing their dishes, hoping and praying Austin would leave it alone.

AUSTIN TRIED to stay out of Lindsey's way for the remainder of the day. It wasn't easy. His three-bedroom home didn't seem nearly as spacious with Lindsay and Josh staying there.

Not that he was complaining. He was grateful she'd allowed him to help this much. He didn't understand why she was so dead set against leaning on him for support. It didn't take a rocket scientist to figure out Sam must have left some debt. As Sam had died on the job, Lindsey should have gotten a nice payment from the company's life insurance policy.

Enough of a settlement that she wouldn't have needed to sell the house and move.

He scowled, wishing he'd known about her financial difficulties. He never should have backed off. But then again, he'd never imagined she'd been forced to move either. All this time he'd been imagining her and Josh living in their nice house, getting back into their normal routine. He had seen her in the emergency department a few times over the past two months but had kept it light, asking how she was, without getting too personal.

Concern nagged at him as he made phone calls, leaving messages with several contractors about Lindsey's home. If he had his way, he'd put the stupid thing on the market. She and Josh could live with him until they got back on their feet.

He winced. Yeah, sure. Like she'd allow that to happen. Not. *Give it up, Monroe.*

"Do you have laundry that needs to be done?" Lindsay stood in the doorway of the living room. "Our clothes smell like smoke."

"Ah, sure." *Do not imagine Lindsey touching your boxers*, he told himself sternly, as he fetched the laundry from the hamper in the bathroom. "Are you sure you don't mind?"

"Why should I?" She gave a careless shrug. "May as well combine loads."

She acted as if doing his laundry was no big deal, but in all the years since he'd left home no woman had ever done his laundry. Sharing that sort of chore seemed more intimate than it should. And the awkwardness between them was driving him crazy. He wished she would relax, but it seemed as though Lindsey was constantly in motion, doing one thing or another.

When Josh returned from skateboarding, Austin suggested they go out and grab a bite to eat. At first Lindsey looked like she was about to argue but then she nodded in agreement.

He took them to a nearby family restaurant, unsure of what kind of food, other than pizza, Josh liked to eat. Apparently he had chosen well when Josh grew excited over the variety of menu options.

"The new subdivision across the street from our old house is awesome for skateboarding," Josh said after the waitress had taken their order. "You should see the houses, Mom, they're really cool."

Lindsey simply smiled and nodded. "I'm glad you and Tony had fun. What else did you do besides skateboarding?"

"We hung out at his house—he has the newest video game and it's so sweet..." his voice trailed off and suddenly he slouched in his seat, picking up his plastic cup of soda and holding it in front of his face.

Austin glanced around to see what had caused Josh's

sudden change from chatterbox to mute. He caught sight of a police officer in full uniform sliding into a booth not far from theirs with his son, who looked to be about Josh's age. He frowned. A friend from school? Or maybe an enemy, since Josh didn't look happy to see him.

"Sit up, straight." Lindsay scolded with an annoyed frown. "Don't spill."

Josh sat up a fraction of an inch and continued to blow bubbles into his glass with a straw. Austin could tell he was hoping the other kid wouldn't see him.

"What's your favorite subject in school?" He thought it was time to change the subject. He edged his chair over, hopefully obstructing the kids view of Josh from the booth.

"I don't know." Josh shrugged, still slouching in his seat.

"Come on, you must have a favorite," Austin urged. "English? Math? History? Science?"

"Math is okay, I guess."

Lindsey glanced at him in surprise. "Just okay? What are you talking about? You love math."

Josh didn't answer as the waitress chose that moment to bring their food.

As they ate, Josh didn't say more than two words unless asked. Austin wondered what was up with Josh and the cop's son, but decided he'd wait until he and Josh were alone to ask.

Lindsey didn't seem to notice Josh's silence. Would she resent his interference if he asked Josh what was going on? Or would she remind him that Josh wasn't his concern? He didn't want her to get angry at him again. Or worse pack up and leave.

Lindsey and Josh shouldn't be alone. Sam should have been there with them.

Sam's death had been his fault. Over these past few

months, the truth had been gnawing at him. Sometime soon, he needed to confess to Lindsey how he had been the cause of Sam's death.

———

"LINDSEY, your next patient has been placed in room six."

"Thanks." She flashed a quick smile at the charge nurse and glanced at the clock hanging over the main electronic census board, amazed to realize her shift was nearly over. These short six hour fill-in shifts were wonderful, especially while Josh was in school.

But then her smile faded as the reality of her situation set in. Short shifts were nice, but she really needed to pick up more hours to pay for homeowners' insurance. Yet with all the trouble Josh had gotten into over these past few months, the thought of leaving him home alone even for another hour or so bothered her. She'd prided herself on always being home for him.

Shaking off her troubled thoughts, she read the name listed beside bed six and the emergency department census board where the patients' names automatically lit up the moment they were registered in triage. Her assigned patient was Blaine Larson, a sixteen-year-old with a possible concussion he had sustained during a fistfight.

"Great," she murmured under her breath. "I hope this isn't where Josh is headed." Skipping school and arguments in the playground were bad enough—she couldn't take it if Josh started fighting.

With a sigh she logged into the computer to read through the initial information the triage nurse had collected. Blaine was awake and alert but only oriented to his name and place. He was confused about the date and time. Otherwise, his vital signs were stable.

After logging off the computer, she grabbed her stethoscope and headed into the room. Blaine was a tall, broadshouldered and nice-looking kid. He had a large welt on his lower lip, but no other outward signs of trauma. With closed head injuries though, the worst part of the damage was hidden from the naked eye.

"Hi, Blaine, my name is Lindsey. I'll be your nurse. Can you tell me what happened?"

"I don't remember. From what I've been told, me and some of my friends were arguing with a couple of jerk football players and one of them slugged me in the face."

"Hmm." She glanced over at her patient's mother seated next to him then looked back at Blaine. "Can you answer a few questions for me? What's your full name?"

"Blaine Michael Larson."

"What day is it?"

"I don't know." He glanced at his mother for help. Lindsey shook her head, indicating his mother shouldn't answer.

"Do you know what month it is?" Lindsey persisted.

"Uh, July? No, wait, August."

Not even close. She frowned. "What about the year? Do you know what year it is?"

"No." Blame rubbed his jaw. "All I know is that someone hit me in the face".

"Where are you now? What is this place?" Lindsey asked.

"A hospital. Sun Valley Community hospital."

"That's right." She smiled, taking a pen light from her pocket and flashing it in the boy's eyes. His pupils looked equal and reactive to light. They weren't overly dilated or misshapen. "Does your head hurt?"

"Not really." He frowned and gently fingered his swollen lip. "Not as bad as my mouth. It really hurts."

"I'm sure it does." She glanced at Blaine's mother. "Do you know if he lost consciousness?"

"Yes, apparently for a few seconds he did." The woman's sighed. "I don't know why he was involved in a fight, he normally gets along fine with people."

She nodded, thinking the same thing about Josh. In the past he'd gotten along fine with other kids at school. Only lately he'd been complaining of stomach aches in the morning. And his grades were slipping, no doubt a result of skipping school. With everything that happened after losing Sam, her son was turning into a complete stranger.

And she didn't know how to get him back.

"Okay, I need to listen to his heart and lungs. Then we'll have the doctor come take a look. He may want to get a CT scan of your son's head, just to make sure everything is alright."

"I understand," Mrs. Larson said.

Lindsey performed a quick assessment but other than his lack of memory Blaine appeared to be a healthy sixteen-year-old. After documenting her findings, she went out to discuss the case with the emergency department physician.

The physician on duty was Dr. Markham. He examined Blaine Larson and then ordered blood work and a CT scan of his head.

"What about a drug screen?" Lindsey asked. "I know he's only sixteen, but shouldn't we check, just in case?"

"That's a good idea. I'll ask his mother." Dr. Markham took Blaine's mother out of the room, and after a brief conversation he returned. "Yes. We're going to add a urine drug and alcohol screen. She said she's never caught him doing any drugs or drinking, but it's best to make sure."

"Will do." Lindsey called the radiology department to arrange the CT scan of his head, then quickly went into draw Blaine's blood. Per Dr. Markham's orders, she was to place a twenty-gauge capped IV in his antecubital vein. "You're going to feel a poke here," she warned.

"Ouch," he yelped when she slid the needle in.

"All done." She drew blood off the line then taped the catheter in place and flushed it with normal saline in case they needed the IV access later. "One of our techs will be here shortly to take you to radiology. We're going to get pictures of your brain to make sure there's no bleeding in there."

"Alright." Blaine was pretty cooperative, considering the gaps in his memory. Some head injury patients could get very aggressive.

She checked on her other patients, one was an elderly man who was waiting to be admitted to a hospital bed for management of his congestive heart failure and the other a young girl who'd broken her wrist falling out of a tree. All in all, a quiet day as far as shifts in the emergency department went.

She took five minutes to eat a sandwich she'd brought from Austin's house, while Blaine was getting his scan. Hopefully, she and Josh would be able to move back home soon. It was sweet of Austin to lend them a hand, but sharing his house was much harder than she'd imagined.

Even worse was the deep temptation to let Austin solve her problems. She knew he would not hesitate to do whatever she asked, if she so much as dropped a hint.

No. She needed to be strong. When she caught a glimpse of Blaine being wheeled back to his room, she jumped up to meet with him. A quick glance in the chart revealed the results were negative. She checked on his laboratory work too, before heading over to talk to Dr. Markham again.

"Labs and radiology reports on Blaine Larson have come back negative." She tapped the computer in front of him. "You can check them for yourself. Even his drug screen is negative."

"That's good to hear. He'd fine to be discharged home, but his mother needs to keep an eye on him for the next twenty-four hours.

She nodded. "Blaine's after visit summary will include care of concussion patients." Their system was set up to pull that information together automatically. This was one of those instances in which upgrading to a new computer system had helped save them time, at least from the nurse's perspective.

She had just finished giving Blaine's mother his after-visit summary, reviewing the care of concussion patient, when she heard her name being called.

"Lindsey? You have a call on line two from Sun Valley elementary school."

The school? Josh? Her stomach knotted as she hurried over to pick up the phone. "This is Lindsey Winters."

"Mrs. Winters? Eric Dolan, principal of Saint Sun Valley school. We have Josh in our office. He's been caught skipping school again. You'll need to come in."

Not again. She closed her eyes and rubbed her temple. What was wrong with him? This was the second time this month. Then a week before that she'd been called because Josh had used foul language on the playground. Her sweet son, using bad language. She could hardly believe it. "I'm at work, as a nurse in the emergency department, but I'll do my best to arrange coverage for my patients so I can get there."

"We'll be waiting." Principal Dolan didn't sound sympathetic.

Feeling sick, Lindsey sought out the charge nurse. "I'm sorry, I need to go. Josh is in trouble. Again."

Sue glanced at the clock. "Well, your shift is over in forty-five minutes anyway, I guess we can cover your patients."

"Thank you." Lindsey gave a quick status update on her remaining patients to other nurses, then left the hospital. Outside in her car, she hesitated, thinking about Austin. As much as she wanted to remain independent, there was no denying Josh needed someone to talk to. Maybe even a father figure. She'd noticed how Austin had tried to draw Josh out over dinner last night attempting to break her son's bad mood.

For a moment she rested her forehead on the steering wheel. Austin was the last man she should lean on for strength. He was far too appealing. Too nice. Too attractive.

Too single!

He was just being nice with his repeated offers to help. And she understood. He was doing this because he was Sam's friend and wanted to look after her. Yet she knew he had a reputation throughout the emergency department of being a bit of a womanizer going from one nurse to the next. She had no interest standing in line for her turn.

If he was interested, which she knew he wasn't. And he hadn't done anything to encourage her attraction to him. He thought she was the grieving widow. He had no idea how strained things had gotten between her and Sam before his death.

She knew Sam's death was her fault. Her husband had probably been upset and not thinking clearly while fighting that wildfire because she'd told him she'd filed for divorce and had asked him to move out, right before he'd left on that last smoke jumping mission.

# CHAPTER THREE

Austin was standing in Lindsey 's house, assessing the water damage in the corner of her living room, when his phone rang. Recognizing her number, he quickly answered. "Hello? Lindsey? Is something wrong?"

"Austin, I'm so sorry to bother you but I need your help." Her voice sounded thick, as if she was crying. "I just received a call from the school. Josh is in trouble."

He frowned; Josh had seemed perfectly fine yesterday. Well, except for his odd withdrawal at dinner. "What happened?"

"He was picked up by the police for skipping school, again," she admitted.

"Skipping school?" Again? Why hadn't she said anything about the first time?

"Yes." She sniffled loudly. "It started a couple months ago, right after we moved. He's skipped school at least three times and I was also called because he used bad language on the playground. I don't know what has gotten into him. He won't talk to me, but I wondered if you might have better luck. Would you mind talking to him?"

He didn't hesitate. "Absolutely. I'll leave now."

"Good. Thanks." She sounded relieved.

"I'll meet you at the school." He pocketed his cell phone and then glanced at the contractor he'd hired to go over Lindsey 's house. "I want a full report within the hour on what needs to be completed to bring this place up to code."

"Will do," the contractor agreed.

Satisfied, he left Lindsey's house and jumped into his truck. The elementary school in Sun Valley wasn't too far, although the house Lindsey had shared with Sam had been much closer. Pushing the speed limit as much as he dared, he made it to the school within fifteen minutes. He parked next to Lindsey's bright yellow car and walked into the building searching for the principal's office.

He instinctively knew where it was. He had spent a few hours in the principal's office when he'd been a kid, too. Not in California, though, but back in Milwaukee Wisconsin where he'd grown up with his siblings.

He found Lindsey was already there, wearing her green hospital scrubs, her arm looped around Josh's thin shoulders. The kid stared down at the floor, as if he wished he could just disappear.

"Mrs. Winters, surely you understand that this behavior has to stop," the principal was saying. "This is the fourth incident over the past two months. Joshua's grades have deteriorated, and if you don't figure out a way to keep him from skipping school, I'm afraid he will need to repeat the fourth grade."

"I understand." Lindsey's desperate gaze sought his. Austin's stomach squeezed in sympathy. First Sam's death, then moving to a new house, then the fire and now this. He had a feeling she couldn't take much more.

"Have you taken our advice and arranged counseling for Josh? "The principal asked in a perplexed tone.

Austin was surprised when she nodded. "Yes." She glanced at Josh, who stared stubbornly at the toes of his shoes. "Dr. Ellen Sandberg is convinced that Josh's anger and lack of interest in school is directly related to the loss of his father."

Austin hadn't known about Josh seeing a psychologist. What else didn't he know? There was a lot Lindsey had kept from him.

"Hmm." The principal's expression was serious. "That may be, and of course, we're very sorry for your loss. I'm sure this is a difficult time for both of you. But Josh is certainly old enough to understand right from wrong, and skipping school is wrong." The principal spread his hands in a help-less gesture. "I'm not sure what you expect us to do. We can't pass him if he doesn't attend school."

"I know that." Austin noticed how Lindsey's grip tighten on Josh's shoulder. "He won't do it again."

When Josh hunched his shoulders and stubbed his toe into the floor, Austin wasn't convinced.

"Josh?" He stepped forward joining the conversation. "What happened? Why did you skip school?"

The boy shrugged and glanced up at him, defiance reflected in his blue eyes. "I don't know."

"*I don't know* is not an acceptable answer," Lindsey said in a sharp tone. "How do you expect to pass if you don't go to school?"

He understood Lindsey's frustration, but there had to be more going on here. Did Josh miss Sam that much? His gut clenched. He hadn't lost his father, so he couldn't even begin to imagine how Josh was coping. Was the boy lonely? Josh had mentioned not having friends nearby, although he had spent the day with Tony. Austin had grown up in a rowdy, noisy family with several brothers and sisters. He'd never been lonely, even when he'd wanted to be left alone.

"Josh will need to serve a detention. And make up the work he's missed," the principal continued. "You'll have to talk to his teacher to arrange for the completion of all missing assignments."

Austin could see that all this talk about extra homework was only making Josh feel worse. Not that he shouldn't do the work, obviously it needed to be completed. But there was no sense dwelling on it.

"Let's go," he spoke in a low tone to Lindsey.

She nodded, understanding his desire to speak with Josh outside of the school. She turned to the principal. "I will be in touch with Josh's teacher."

The principal stood. "Ms. Winters, I'd like to receive a report from his counselor prior to allowing Josh back into class. I need to know there is something more going on here with Josh's truancy."

"Okay." Lindsey's worried frown brought a wave of helpless anger washing over him. She shouldn't have to bear the burden of all of this alone. She needed help and support to get through this. She tugged Josh's arm. "Let's go."

Josh followed her out, looking completely dejected. Austin felt bad for the kid. What in the world had happened? There had to be a reason he was acting like he was. Because of the move? It didn't seem like a simple move would be enough to cause him to skip school. Josh had always been a nice kid, had never been in trouble before that Austin was aware of.

"I'm sorry to bother you," Lindsey said as they walked through the parking lot to their respective cars. They'd managed to stay out of each other 's way that morning as she'd gotten Josh up and ready for school and then left for work. But now they were walking closely together.

"It's not a big deal. I was at your house talking to the contractor." He glanced at Josh, who lagged behind as if he didn't want to be near either of the adults. "We'll meet at my place, okay? I'd like to try talking to Josh alone."

She nodded and he figured it was a sign of how upset she was that she didn't jump on his comment about the contractor. "Do you think he'll talk to you, Austin? So far, Dr. Sandberg hasn't had much luck."

"I don't know, but I'll try." He opened the driver side car door for her. When she leaned close to slide in behind the wheel, her subtle scent teased his senses. He hoped he hid his reaction to her well enough that she wouldn't notice.

He'd tried to keep his distance from her, but that was much harder to achieve when they were living together under the same roof.

She hesitated, placing her hand over his on the top of the car door. His pulse leapt at the light touch. "I'd really appreciate you talking to him. I just don't understand what has gotten into him over these past few months."

For a moment he stared at their hands, wishing he could pull her close, but then she turned away. Josh climbed into the passenger seat and was staring sullenly out the window. Austin took a deep breath, forcing himself to maintain control.

"I'll see you at... my place." He'd almost said *home*. As if Lindsey and Josh belonged there with him. Giving himself a mental shake, he closed the car door and waited until she pulled out before sliding into his truck to follow.

The ride to his house was short. He pulled into the driveway, parking beside Lindsey 's vehicle. He strode inside, finding Lindsey and Josh seated in the living room.

Josh stared at the floor again, looking miserable, and Lindsey didn't appear to be feeling much better. He hated the deep grooves of worry around her eyes.

She rose to her feet when she saw him. "I'll let you guys talk while I throw in some laundry." She caught herself and looked at him askance. "If you don't mind?"

"Of course not," he hastened to reassure her. The last thing he wanted was for her to feel like a guest. He would rather she be comfortable. "I told you to make yourself at home."

She nodded and disappeared down the hall toward the laundry room. He didn't think she'd appreciate knowing how much he liked having her there to share the house-keeping chores. To be honest, he wouldn't have minded doing most of the work himself, as long as she stayed with him. Tearing his mind from those ridiculous thoughts, he turned to look at Josh. He gestured to the vacant spot on the sofa. "Do you mind if I sit down?"

The kid shrugged without making eye contact. Austin purposefully sat next to him, trying to think of a way to get the boy to open up. "I think I know what you're going through."

"Yeah, right," Josh muttered. "You don't."

"I do," he repeated. "I know you miss your dad very much. I guess school doesn't seem very important right now, does it?"

Josh shook his head. "No. It's not."

"Are the kids teasing you? Or are you just sad over missing your dad?"

Josh was quiet for so long he was afraid the boy wouldn't answer. When he finally spoke, Austin had to lean forward in order to hear him. "The first time I left school, struggling over missing my dad, Bobby's dad caught me. Bobby's been making fun of me ever since."

The cop's son? Remembering the kid and his dad in the restaurant last night, Josh's strange behavior made sense. He and Bobby obviously had a history.

"Bobby has no right to make fun of you, but continuing to skip school isn't going to help." He paused, then asked, "Did Bobby's dad find you again, today?"

Josh nodded, his face grim.

That figured. Austin leaned forward. "Look, Josh, I know school seems stupid right now, but you have to pull yourself together. The last thing you need right now is to fail your classes. You don't want to repeat fourth grade, that will only cause more teasing. Do you think your dad would want you to skip school?"

"No." Josh hunched his shoulders again, as if he wanted to curl into a ball. "But sometimes I'm so sad I can't stand it. I leave school because I don't want any of the other kids to see me cry."

Oh, man. He could completely understand. He wrapped his arm around Josh's thin shoulders. "Josh, I cried when your dad died. It's nothing to be ashamed of."

Josh swiped his face against his arm and sniffled loudly. "I just miss him."

"I know you do." He held on to Josh tightly, wishing more than anything he'd been the one to die that day instead of Sam. "I miss him, too."

For a long moment they hung onto each other, sharing their grief. He glanced over to see Lindsey working in the kitchen, keeping busy. These past few months must have been just as hard on her.

"Why don't you tell your mom about this?" He asked, when Josh finally pushed away.

"I don't want her to feel sad, too. She always looks like she's gonna cry when I talk about my dad."

Josh was protecting his mom. Austin couldn't say anything—he probably would have done the same thing.

"I wish I didn't have to see Bobby at school tomorrow," Josh muttered.

"I know it's not easy, but you have to learn to ignore Bobby," Austin said firmly. "He's just a kid. There must be some way to avoid him."

Josh shrugged. "I've tried to stay away, but he always finds me. Then he's mean to me."

"Is that when you were caught using bad language on the playground?" Austin surmised.

"Yeah."

Bobby sounded like a bit of a bully. Josh needed something to help take his mind off missing his dad. "Okay, Josh, we need to find something to keep you busy. Do you like sports?"

"Sort of," Josh said without enthusiasm. "I like to skateboard but I'm not all that good."

Austin racked his brain, trying to think. Bobby was probably into sports, so Josh needed something different. He remembered the Tai Kwon Do studio he had passed on his way to the elementary school. "What about learning martial arts?"

Josh perked up. "That might be cool."

So far, so good. "I'll talk to your mom about this. But Josh, you really need to stay in school. Just avoid Bobby and his friends. Getting your grades up has to be your top priority."

"Can Tony learn Tai Kwon Do with me?" Josh asked.

"Yes, but the deal is that your grades cannot suffer. Understood?" He wasn't sure this idea would go over well with Lindsey, especially considering her financial difficulties, but he'd do his best to convince her. Josh needed something to focus on, something that would help him deal with missing his dad. The martial arts were all about being spiritually strong, as well as physically strong. He thought maybe it could work. "I'll talk to your mom and see if we can work out a schedule that works for you and Tony to take classes together."

"Cool." For the first time since seeing Josh sitting in the principal's office, he saw a spark of interest flare in the boy's eyes.

"Just remember, your grades must improve," Austin warned. "Homework has to come first."

"I know." Josh nodded eagerly. "I can pull up my grades, they're not that bad." When Austin raised a disbelieving brow, the boy's chin dropped to his chest and he added, "Well, maybe they are bad, but I'll make up all my missing assignments."

"I'm glad to hear it." He wanted to believe Josh could pull himself together. "And I'm here if you ever want to talk about your dad."

"Okay."

Austin stood, glancing toward the kitchen to where Lindsey was busy with folding laundry on the kitchen table. She looked so beautiful, with her blonde hair falling in waves to her shoulders, that he had to physically steel himself against the need to pull her close. "I'd like you to get started on those missing assignments right now, while I talk to your mom."

Josh frowned. "Are you gonna tell her why I've been skipping school?"

He hesitated, not wanting to break the boy's trust. Yet at the same time he didn't want to lie to Lindsey either. "Josh,

I'm sure your mom understands how much you miss your dad."

"But I don't want her to be sad, too," Josh protested.

Austin understood the boy didn't want to contribute to her grief. "I know, but she loves you and needs to know where you're going to be alright. Telling her might help her agree to send you to Tai Kwon Do classes."

Josh grimaced but then nodded. "Okay," he grudgingly agreed.

Austin turned toward the kitchen, wishing he felt as confident as he sounded. Unease tightened his gut.

He and Lindsey needed to talk about more than just the repairs on her house. Josh needed someone to talk to, someone he could relate to. Austin wanted to be there for both of them.

He needed to fulfill his promise to Sam.

There had to be a way to convince her to let him help.

---

LINDSEY WAS grateful Dr. Ellen Sandberg had returned her phone call so quickly. She nodded at Austin when he came into the kitchen and continued her conversation. "I need to make an appointment for Josh, as soon as possible. He skipped school again and they won't let him back into class until you see him and provide an update on his progress."

"I could probably squeeze him in later this afternoon, say about five o'clock?" Dr. Sandberg offered.

"Five would be great. Thank you so much." Relieved she disconnected from the call. Austin's presence in the kitchen made it seem smaller than normal.

She was keenly aware of how Austin intently watched

her as she folded a load of clothes. She flushed under his scrutiny and hoped he'd blame her red cheeks on the heat from the dryer.

"I would like to go with him," he said.

"With whom?" Flustered, she glanced at him. "Oh, you mean with Josh? To his psychologist's appointment?"

"Yeah." Austin tucked his hands into the front pockets of his jeans. "I'd like to go with him to see Dr. Sandberg. At five, right?"

Surprised, she stared at him. She couldn't believe he was offering to go with Josh. When things had started going downhill between her and Sam, she'd suggested marriage counseling, but Sam had flatly refused to attend. He hadn't believed there had was anything counseling could do to change things between them.

"I—uh—don't see why not. Although we'd have to get Dr. Sandberg's approval." She glanced away, wishing Austin wasn't so appealing. He looked great even wearing nothing more than a casual T-shirt and well-worn denim jeans. He smelled amazing, too. For a moment she remembered how he'd stood at her side throughout Sam's funeral. It had taken every ounce of willpower she'd possessed not to lean on his rugged strength. To keep him at a safe distance.

She wasn't a pathetic widow who needed a man to get by. Sam hadn't deserved to die, but she'd already planned to live her life without him. Jumping into a relationship with another man wasn't part of the plan. No matter how difficult things were, she wasn't about to follow in her mother's footsteps, leaping headfirst into a new relationship the moment the previous one ended. Lindsey had suffered through three stepfathers, not to mention several boyfriends in between.

None of the men her mother had hooked up with had been a contender for father of the year.

"Here, let me help." He crossed over and pitched in, picking up a shirt and folding it. She subtly edged sideways, trying to give him more room. The muscles of his arms rippled with the simple movement, and she remembered the day Austin had come to help Sam fix the leaky roof. He'd stripped off his shirt, displaying the bronze muscles of his shoulders and chest to full advantage.

Not that Sam had been a wimp, but for all Austin's strength there had always been a gentleness about him, as well. A soft caring side that her husband had seemed to lose somewhere along the ten-year course of their marriage.

Stop dwelling on the worst, she told herself sternly. Sam wasn't a bad guy, there had just been something... missing. Sam was gone, there was no reason to dwell on what had failed in their marriage.

Austin looked good, whether he was doing housework or repairing the roof. Yet she knew it wasn't fair to compare Austin to Sam. She needed to focus on Josh, not her inappropriate response to her husband's best friend.

Besides, even if she had been in the market for a man, Austin wasn't her type. She knew Austin never lacked female company. Even Sam had mentioned how single women flocked to his friend. He'd claimed Austin never dated the same woman twice. She'd often suspected Sam had been jealous because Austin had been single and Sam wasn't.

Thank heavens she wasn't looking for a relationship, or she might have been come obsessed with Austin too.

Annoyed with herself, she finished folding the laundry and stepped back. "We should probably consider an easy dinner, as Josh has his appointment at five."

"Lindsey—" he began, but then halted when his phone rang. He lifted the device to his ear. "Hi Mark. Tell me what you found."

She listened, belatedly realizing Austin was talking to the contractor about her house. He'd mentioned being there earlier, but she'd been so upset over Josh that it really hadn't registered in her brain.

The serious expression settling over Austin's features was not reassuring.

"Thanks Mark. I'll discuss the situation with the owner and get back to you." He lowered his phone and glanced at her.

"What's wrong?"

"Did you buy the house from a realtor?" He asked.

"No, I bought it directly from the owner. Why?"

"The electrical wiring isn't up to code. And the water damage from your neighbor's fire means you also need to replace the drywall in the living room, and likely replace some of the insulation in the attic." His expression was grim. "It's going to take a few weeks to get your house into shape before you and Josh can move back in."

Stunned, she dropped into the closest kitchen chair, her knees weak. Surely, he was exaggerating. "Weeks?" She echoed.

"Yes. I'm sorry. Lindsey, I'd like to help. I don't want to steal your independence, but I need to know you and Josh are safe. Plus, I think Josh could really use a male role model right now to help keep him in school." He dropped to his knees beside her chair and caught her hands, his gaze imploring. "Will you please consider moving in with me temporarily? Just until your house repairs are complete."

# CHAPTER FOUR

"Move in with you?" Lindsey stared at him, hardly able to comprehend what he was saying. Move in with Austin? So that two of them would be together all the time? Did he have any idea what he was asking of her? She pulled out of his grip, reining in her turbulent emotions. "No. I'm sorry, but I can't."

"Why not?" He didn't get angry or upset but looked truly puzzled. "Are you afraid I'll get in your way? I promise you'll have all the privacy you need." An odd expression flickered across his face. "Are you seeing someone? Is that it?"

"What?" She almost burst out laughing and quickly covered the strangled sound with a cough. "No. I'm not remotely interested in seeing anyone." Bad enough that she was attracted to him.

"Then why won't you let me help?" His brows drew together in a frown. "This is what friends are for, to support each other in difficult times."

She sighed. Friends. Austin had been Sam's friend, not hers. Sure they'd chatted when they bumped into each other at work, but it wasn't as if they'd had deeply personal conversations or anything. How could she think of Austin as a friend, when every moment she was with him she was hyper aware of him as a man? Impossible. She lifted her chin. "If I were a man, you wouldn't be inviting me to move in with you. But because I'm a helpless female with a young son, then I must need your support, right?"

Austin was quiet for a long moment. "Lindsay, you couldn't be further from the truth. I don't see you as a help- less female at all. You're a wonderful, smart, caring emer- gency nurse. I respect you more than I can say. But think about Josh for a minute. He's obviously going through some difficult times. I got him to open up a little just now, and he is having trouble coping with Sam's death. Don't you think staying here for a little while might be better for him?"

She opened her mouth to argue then closed it again without uttering a word. He'd effectively pointed out the one concern she couldn't argue against. Josh would always come first. And she was thrilled he'd opened up to Austin. Maybe her son did need a male role model right now. If she were honest, she'd admit there wasn't a better guy for the job than, Austin.

Still, she wavered. Hadn't her mother often used the same excuse? *We need to move in with Richard because we can't afford to pay our rent. I'm doing this for you, Lindsay. Trust me, I know what I'm doing.*

"No strings, Lindsay," Austin was saying as if reading her thoughts. "I promise I only want to help. Why don't you try staying here, just for a week or so, and see how it goes? A trial run, if that helps. That way, if this arrangement it doesn't work out, you aren't obligated to stay. I'll help you move into a hotel."

And he would. Deep in her heart she knew that much.

If she insisted on going to a hotel right now, he'd take her. She knew Austin wasn't like all those men her mother had hooked up with after her father had taken off, leaving them with a heavy mortgage, not unlike the debt Sam had left behind. The men her mother had married hadn't been horribly abusive or anything, her mother hadn't been that far gone. But moving in with one guy after another had been difficult.

Ten years ago, she'd thought Sam had been so different. Settled. Dependable. As it had turned out, he'd been much more like her father than she realized. Which only made her that much more determined not to be like her mother.

"I don't know," she hedged, wishing she had another option. The memory of the Tolliver's fire was still front and center in her mind. As much as she wanted to be independent, she wasn't willing to put her son's safety at risk, either. If Austin said the wiring wasn't up to code, she believed him. "I'm worried about how this may affect Josh. I don't want him to think we're—uh..." she trailed off, embarrassed. "I think it's fair to say he'll look at you as a surrogate father. I don't want him to feel lost all over again when we have to move back home," she amended.

"You need to understand, I'm not about to drop out of Josh's life no matter where you decide to live." His keen green gaze held hers. "I'd like to stay involved if you'll let me. Think of me as Josh's big brother."

His offer was illogical. Tempting. Could she do this? Could she live with Austin while keeping her attraction a secret?

This wasn't about her, but about Josh. No question she would suffer through anything for her son's sake.

Praying she wasn't taking the easy way out, she slowly nodded. "Alright, I'll agree to a trial period to see how things go. But it would be nice if we could get the repairs done on my house as quickly as possible."

"Sure thing." Relief flooded his features and he grinned. "Thanks. You won't regret this, I promise." His brilliantly white grin did funny things to her stomach. She managed a weak smile in return, hoping he was right.

But deep down she suspected there would be some point in the not-so-distant future that she'd look back on this moment with regret.

---

WHILE AUSTIN and Josh went to see Dr. Sandberg, she busied herself with making dinner. She didn't go crazy trying to impress Austin, since she was no expert in the kitchen, but threw together a simple spaghetti meal.

Still, she felt a warm glow when Austin sniffed the air with obvious appreciation when they returned. "Wow. Something smells amazing."

"It's no big deal." She downplayed the domesticity of the moment, although she keenly felt the intimacy shimmering between them. "Like you said at breakfast yesterday, I had to make dinner for Josh, anyway. I simply made enough to share."

"Thank you." His simple acceptance helped make her feel less self-conscious. This living together stuff was going to take some getting used to.

The three of them sat down at the table, and she was surprised when Austin said, "If you don't mind, I'd like to say grace."

Really? That wasn't something Sam had ever done. "Of course." She hid her flushed cheeks by bowing her head.

"Dear Lord, we thank You for this food we are about to

eat. We also ask that You continue to guide us on Your chosen path. Amen."

"Amen," she murmured. Was being here with Austin part of God's chosen path? She wasn't sure.

"Do you always pray," Josh asked.

"When I remember," Austin said with a smile.

They ate in silence for a few minutes. She glanced at him, expectantly, and he nodded, realizing she wanted him to broach the subject of their living arrangements.

"Josh, we need to discuss a few things," Austin said. "It looks like you and your mom will have to stay here for a while. Your house sustained a fair amount of water damage after your neighbor's fire. Your mom agreed that it would be best if you both stayed here until the repairs are complete."

"Really?" Josh's bright blue eyes, so much like Sam's, flashed with hope. "That is so cool!"

"It's a temporary arrangement," she warned. "A couple of weeks at the most."

"I know," Josh said with a grin. She suspected a couple of weeks seemed like forever to a nine-year-old. "I can't wait to tell Tony."

Since Tony lived just a few blocks away, she understood Josh's enthusiasm. His response reassured her that she'd made the right decision. Maybe these few weeks wouldn't be so bad. Anything to help turn Josh around from the stranger he'd been to the boy she'd once known.

"Lindsey, I was thinking it would be good for Josh to learn Tai Kwon Do."

"What?" She froze, her fork halfway to her mouth as she swung her gaze back to Austin. "Are you crazy? Why would you suggest something like that?" She was seriously annoyed. Why on earth had he brought this up in front of

Josh? Had Austin done it on purpose, so that she could be the bad guy when she had to say no?

Once again, Austin was interfering in the way she raised her son.

"Tai Kwon Do is all about self-discipline which is a trait that can be applied to many things, like homework." Austin finished his spaghetti and then surprised her by standing and clearing away the dirty dishes. "The whole focus of martial arts is all about teaching self-control."

Oh sure. She was supposed to believe that? And her obvious skepticism, he continued, "Seriously, I wouldn't have suggested it if I didn't think it would help. I ran the idea past Dr. Sandberg and she thought it would be good for Josh, too. And you don't have to worry about the cost—consider this an early birthday present from me to Josh."

"Please, Mom?" Her son's gaze implored her to agree. "I promise I will do better in school."

She sighed, glancing between the two of them, wondering if she was the one being unreasonable. She wanted to refuse on principle, because Austin was interfering again. Especially since taking Austin's money for something like this went against the grain.

Yet hadn't she asked for his help when Josh had skipped school? What if she was wrong? If Dr. Sandberg had considered this a good idea, learning Tai Kwon Do could be just what Josh needed. When was the last time she'd seen Josh looked so excited?

Months. Since before Sam's death.

Wavering, she slowly nodded. "Okay, I'll approve the Tai Kwon Do lessons. But Josh? If you skip school or get into another argument with the other kids on the playground, I'll yank you out of those classes so fast your head will spin." It was not an empty threat.

"Yay! Thanks, Mom." Following Austin's example, Josh picked up his empty plate and carried it to the sink.

"Finish your homework," Austin said in a stern tone.

Josh nodded and ran to his room. For a moment she was irritated with Austin's seemingly effortless ability to get her son to listen.

Then was ashamed of herself for resenting him. After all, wasn't the need for a father figure exactly why she'd agreed to this temporary arrangement? She should be grateful Austin cared enough about Josh to be there for him.

"Thank you," Austin said softly. "I think learning Tai Kwon Do is just what Josh needs to give him some badly needed self-confidence."

"I hope so." She carried her own dishes to the sink. Then turned to face him. "But next time you'd better run the idea past me first, without involving Josh. I didn't appreciate being put on the spot like that."

He winced at her sharp tone and looked apologetic as he took the soiled plate from her hands. "I'm sorry about that. You're right. I guess I didn't think." He shooed her away from the sink. "You cooked, it's my job to clean up. That's the rule in the Monroe household. Why don't you relax for a few minutes? We'll head back to your house in a little while to get the rest of your things."

Relax? While living in the same house as Austin? Not likely. "It's your night off," she protested. "I'm sure you have better things to do."

"Nope." His tone was cheerful. "Why don't you make a list of whatever you think you'll need over the next couple of weeks? We will hit the road as soon as I'm finished."

She couldn't think of anything they'd need, other than maybe more clothing. Especially work scrubs for her. Austin had pretty much everything else covered here. As she sat at the table, watching him work, she belatedly realized her decision to move in with Austin might cramp his bachelor lifestyle. Hadn't he point blank asked if she was seeing someone? Just because she wasn't interested in a relationship, didn't mean Austin wasn't. This was his night off. Didn't he usually go out in his free time? Based on the gossip within the emergency department he dated often.

And what if he met some woman he wanted to bring home?

A pang of jealousy cramped her stomach, making her feel slightly sick.

"I realize you probably have plans on your evenings off, so don't worry about us," she quickly said, pushing past the lump in her throat. "Josh is usually in bed by nine o'clock on school nights and I'm usually asleep, early too. You don't have to worry about disturbing us or anything." She knew she was babbling but couldn't seem to stop. "I mean really, don't think Josh and I will get in the way of your social life. Just do what you always do and pretend we're not here."

Austin paused in the act of rinsing the dishes and neatly stacking them in the dishwasher to glance at her. "I'm not seeing anyone and haven't for months. Do you honestly think I'd bring a woman home with you and Josh here?"

He hadn't gone out with anyone in months? Secretly relieved, she shrugged. "Why not? This is your home, Austin. And we're just friends."

"Yes, we are, but I'm not interested in a social life, as you so carefully put it." He offered a lopsided grin. "Right now, nothing is more important than you and Josh."

"Okay, but if you change your mind—," she began.

He interrupted. "I won't."

"All right." She smiled, a warm glow sweeping through

her at his words, even though she knew he probably didn't really mean them.

At least, not in the way she wished he did.

———

OVER THE NEXT couple of nights, Austin had trouble sleeping. Three days of living with Lindsey was getting to him. On the third night, he tossed and turned, kicking off the covers. He threw himself on his back, feeling as if his skin was too tight for his body. What was wrong with him? He hadn't felt this wired since the night of the fire.

After an hour, he rolled out of bed and doused himself with cold water, hoping the cool shower would ease his tension. It helped a little, but as he stared at his reflection in the mirror above the sink, he forced himself to admit the hard truth.

His bright idea of supporting Lindsey and Josh was wreaking havoc with his brain. He was so hyper aware of her, noticing every moment she made, the mere scent of her as she passed by. He could only imagine how difficult this would be for the next ten days. Maybe longer.

He sighed and rubbed the back of his neck. He'd just have to get over it. He had the ridiculous notion that focusing on Josh would help keep his desire for Lindsey under control. But Josh was old enough to spend a fair amount of time with his friends, and during those times Josh was gone or otherwise occupied, swimming in the pool out back or playing video games, he and Lindsey were alone. And those stolen moments of togetherness did nothing to help him ignore his growing attraction for her.

Turning away from his rueful reflection, he drew on a clean pair of shorts and stood at the patio doors, gazing out at the pool in the backyard where Josh and Tony had spent a couple of hours earlier that afternoon, playing water volleyball. At least Josh was enjoying his new surroundings. He'd gotten that much right.

He'd gone so far as to consider going out on a date as a distraction but couldn't bring himself to do it. During his most recent trip home over the holidays, he'd learned that other women didn't hold the same appeal they once had. At first he thought it had been because he was grieving Sam's death. Battling the guilt over his role in losing his friend. But then he realized it was more. No matter how hard he tried, he hadn't been able to summer the smallest flicker of interest in another woman. Oh, he'd flirted with Krista Vaughn to make his brother Adam jealous, but he hadn't really wanted to go out with her.

Once he'd dated women whenever the mood struck. But not anymore. He wasn't interested in anyone else.

Only Lindsey.

And that scared the heck out of him.

Unable to bear the closed in feel of his bedroom, he turned and crossed the room. Silently, he opened his door and padded down the hall, passed Lindsey's and Josh's rooms to the kitchen.

He knew his way around without using lights, and his bare feet didn't make a sound as he entered the room. But when he bumped into something soft, he abruptly realized he wasn't alone.

Lindsey let out a soft cry, taking a quick step backward. He reached out and grasped her shoulders to study her.

"You scared me," she whispered in a strangled voice.

"I'm sorry," he said, immediately contrite. He did feel bad about frightening her. But he couldn't find any remorse over being with her alone like this. Even in the dark, she was the vision of his dreams, her blonde hair falling in waves across her shoulders. Her soft lemony scent muddled his brain.

She turned her face away, the flash of moonlight through the window bathing her profile in a soft glow. He sucked in a quick breath when he saw the glint of tears.

"What is it?" He tightened his grip on her slim shoulders. "What happened? What's wrong?"

"Nothing." Her denial was too quick and she brushed away the tears, breaking free of her of his hands to turn away.

He didn't like knowing she had been crying. "Please, tell me what upset you. Is it Josh? Something I said? Something I did? What?"

"No, it's nothing like that." This time, her lips curved in a small smile. "I—had a bad dream, that's all. When you scared me, it came rushing back. It's silly. Don't know why I let a dream get to me."

A bad dream he could handle, he thought although his heart still squeezed at the way she'd been so upset. He lightly touched her arm, then drew her close, offering comfort. "Hey, it's okay. We've all had nightmares at some point."

Expecting her to pull away again, he was surprised when she'd leaned into him, burying her face in the curve of his neck, hanging on as if she never planned to let go.

His heart thudded painfully in his chest and he slid a hand down the curve of her back, acutely aware of her shorts and soft T-shirt she wore as pajamas. The warmth of her skin radiated through the thin cotton. His fingers itched to draw her closer.

When her lips brushed lightly against his neck, he froze,

wondering if he'd imagined the caress. But then, the moisture of her breath fanned his cheek.

"Lindsey?" Mixed signals clamored in his brain. Was this because of the dream? Or was it possible she wanted the same thing he did?

In response, she tipped her head back to look up at him in the darkness. He slowly lowered his head, giving her plenty of time to pull away, before he captured her parted lips with his mouth, claiming her in a bone jarring, mind numbing kiss.

# CHAPTER FIVE

Austin's kiss was so simmering hot, she was surprised her feet didn't melt into the floor.

Rational thought vanished. She should push him away, but the need clamoring through her had other ideas. Instead, she clutched his shoulders and returned his kiss, basking in the thrill of desire. How long had it been since she'd kissed a man?

Eons. Or so it seemed.

Austin didn't just kiss her, he devoured her with his mouth as if nothing was more important than her lips.

Then he abruptly thrust her away, breathing deeply and holding on to the kitchen counter for support. Despite the darkness, she caught a hint of a dazed expression on his face. "I'm sorry. I had no right to cross the line like that."

Bereft, she leaned against the sink her knees threatening to buckle. Why had he stopped? She licked her lips, and it took all her self-control not to throw herself back into his arms.

Bad enough that she'd kissed him. Not the other way around.

"Don't move out," Austin spoke fast as if he was worried she would interrupt. Did he think she was angry with him? A hysterical laugh nearly broke free. "I promise I won't cross the line this way ever again. I never meant to make you feel uncomfortable."

Okay, then. He obviously wanted to keep their relationship on friendly terms. She should be glad because she wasn't in the market for anything more. Yet there was an emptiness inside where love and passion had once been. Until now, she hadn't missed having a man in her life. She swallowed hard and nodded, hoping he couldn't see her blush in the dark.

What if she wanted their amazing kiss to happen again? What if she wanted more than just friendship?

Forget it. What she wanted didn't matter. Austin was a friend. And she knew him well enough to know he wasn't the type of guy who did long term relationships.

"It's all right I—don't worry about it." What could she say? Admit that she wanted that toe curling kiss more than he had? And then what. No as tempting as it sounded, she knew better. In the years she had known him through Sam, she'd never met a steady girlfriend of his. And that was all the proof she needed to know he would not be interested in a long-term relationship with her.

"You won't leave?" His tone was anxious.

"No," she said slowly. "I won't leave." Even though she knew she should.

He was quiet for a moment, before murmuring, "Good. Thank you. Good night, Lindsey. Sweet dreams."

"Good night." Unable to move, she stayed where she was until Austin moved silently back down the hall to his bedroom. Alone again, she let out a heavy sigh and sank into the nearest kitchen chair, willing her heart to return to its normal rhythm.

If she were smart, she would leave. Pack her and Josh's things and move into the nearest hotel. But she couldn't. Truthfully, she couldn't afford a hotel. And Josh needed Austin, more than she'd realized.

No, the only option was for her to find the strength to keep a safe friendly distance between them.

***

LINDSEY MANAGED to stay out of Austin's way over the next few days. Of course, it helped that he seemed to be staying away from her, too.

And while it hurt to realize he was avoiding her, she told herself to get over it. It was better this way.

They mainly spoke during dinner. They'd gotten into the habit of sharing their evening meal each night Austin wasn't working, in a very family-like way. Except Austin insisted on taking turns with the cooking, depending on which one of them happened to get home first. On certain days, like tonight, he drove Josh and his friend Tony to their Tai Kwon Do lessons, so she'd gotten home before he did. She didn't mind cooking for them.

Yet tonight, when he and Josh walked in, she decided it was past time they had a serious discussion about the progress on her home repairs. She'd left the details for Austin to deal with for far too long.

"Something smells delicious," Austin greeted her with a cheerful grin.

She rolled her eyes. He always said that no matter if she made tuna casserole or lasagna. Tonight, she'd thrown together baked chicken. Nothing fancy.

"Thanks. Have a seat, it's ready." When they were all seated around the table she looked at him expectantly, knowing he always said grace.

He flashed a smile, then bowed his head. "Dear Lord Jesus we thank you for this food we are about to eat, and we ask that You keep us on Your chosen path. Amen."

"Amen," she murmured, wondering if God had brought her to Austin on purpose. It seemed that way.

"Amen," Josh added. He'd gotten used to praying, too.

When they were all served, she got to the point. "Austin, you never told me exactly what the repairs would be at my house. I need to know how much this is going to cost me."

He arched a brow. "Don't worry about it, I'll take care of everything."

She ground her teeth at his slightly condescending tone. How many times had she heard that from Sam? Only to discover after his death that he hadn't taken care of anything. "It's my house. I'd like to know exactly what is being done and how much it will cost."

He hesitated as if finally realizing she was dead serious. He slowly nodded. "Okay, sure. I'll get you the paperwork after we finish eating."

She almost pushed for more information now but decided it was better to wait since Josh was sitting there, listening. Slightly mollified, she took a bite of her chicken. Not bad, if she did say so herself.

"Mom, we learned how to do a jumping snap kick today," Josh said in an excited tone. "You should see how high I can kick! I can't wait until we get to break boards with our feet."

She eyed Austin warily. "Break boards with his feet?"

"Yep, but don't worry it's very safe," Austin assured her. "They practice a lot before doing the real thing."

She hoped so. "I'm glad you're enjoying your lessons."

"Will you come watch me when I test out to become a yellow belt?" Josh persisted.

She didn't realize there was a test as part of the process. When Austin gave a slight nod, she hastened to agree. "Sure. I'd love to."

"It won't be for a few weeks yet, but I can't wait." Josh wrinkled his nose. "White belts are for sissies."

"Hey, don't talk like that," Austin chided. "Remember what your sensei told you? There will always be someone worse than you and someone better than you. This is a test of your own strength and endurance, no one else's. You are only competing against yourself."

"Yeah, I know." Josh shrugged. "But I still want to be a yellow belt."

It was amazing to see her son so excited about his classes and hoped this activity would channel his energy into something constructive rather than destructive, like skipping school. The one nice thing about Josh's classes was that they were right after school, so with Austin's help driving him on his days off she'd been able to sign up for a couple extra shifts on the days Josh had class.

She had a feeling she'd need every dime she could earn in order to pay for the repairs.

After Austin cleaned up the dinner dishes, he brought an envelope filled with papers to the kitchen table. He pulled them out and spread them out for her to see. "Here are the quotes I've received and obviously I've accepted the most reasonable ones. The electricians are rewiring the house first, and then I'll arrange for the drywall repairs."

Steeling herself for the worse, she still let out a horrified gasp when she saw the amount of both the wiring and the drywall repairs. "That much?"

Austin nodded. "I'm afraid so. But I'm pretty sure your homeowner's insurance will cover it."

She blinked, hoping she'd imagined those extra zeros on the end of the number, but knew she hadn't. How in the world would she manage to pay that amount?

There was only one answer and that was to take out a home equity loan. Buying the small house outright meant she only had to pay the property taxes each month. It wouldn't be easy to juggle those loan payments in addition to everything else, but she didn't see many options.

Thanks to Sam, her credit rating was horrible. She had made certain every one of his debts had been paid off in full, by selling the house and using most of his life insurance policy. She had put the rest into the small one-bedroom bungalow. But there was still the one outstanding credit card bill that she was only making monthly payments on.

She stared at the amount, feeling foolish. Why hadn't she realized how much this would cost? She stared at her hands, her heart heavy. She wouldn't ask Austin for a loan, she would just have to make sure the home equity loan wouldn't be so high that she wouldn't be able to make the payments.

"Lindsey?" He reached out and took her hand. It was the first time he touched her since that moment of moon-light madness they shared in the kitchen. A kiss that had haunted her ever since. "What is it? What's wrong?"

She had to tell him. As much as she wanted to crawl under a rock and hide, she'd learned the hard way that ignoring her problems would not make them go away.

"I don't have homeowner's insurance." She couldn't bring herself to meet his gaze. "But don't worry, I'll head over to the bank first thing in the morning to apply for a home equity loan."

"You don't have homeowner's insurance?" He repeated in shock. "You did receive Sam's life insurance payout after he died, didn't you?"

"Yes." She was embarrassed to tell him just how badly Sam had gotten them into debt. Especially as she'd been so clueless. Why hadn't she insisted on being involved in paying their bills? Sam used to get so upset when she'd tried to help, that she'd simply backed off.

And she'd almost done the same thing again with the repairs on her house, leaving everything to Austin. When would she learn from her mistakes? She cleared her throat. "You must have figured out things have been difficult for us financially. But it doesn't matter." She forced herself to look him in the eye. "It's my house, Austin. I will pay for the repairs. Thank you for arranging the contractors for me." She tugged her hand from his and stood.

"Lindsey, wait—" he began.

Shaking her head, she walked out, leaving him alone, not wanting to see the flash of pity in his eyes.

---

AUSTIN COULDN'T BELIEVE things had gotten so desperate for Lindsey and Josh. What in the world had Sam done? She said she'd got the life insurance payout but still had been forced to sell her house. And hadn't paid for homeowner's insurance, either.

Thank heavens he'd managed to convince her to move in with him for a while. At least he could help cover the cost of groceries. And using the Tai Kwon Do classes as a birthday present for Josh had been pure genius. He hadn't minded paying for the sessions, along with the V-neck *dobak* Josh wore with pride.

He scrubbed his hands over his face. During the day he managed to keep busy enough to stay out of Lindsey's way. He'd wanted her for a long time, but first she'd belonged to Sam and now she was still grieving Sam's death. No matter how hard he tried to talk himself out of wanting her, his hormones had other ideas. He couldn't forget their kiss, the burning memory lingering.

He'd crossed the line—had allowed his stupid desire to ruin their friendship. And he really missed their easy camaraderie. He'd berated himself over and over again for losing control, for allowing physical desire to override his common sense.

Yet, no matter what, he couldn't forget that she hadn't been the one to break off the embrace. He had. What would have happened if he hadn't have stopped? He hadn't imagined the way she'd responded to his embrace, kissing him back.

Unless she'd pretended that he'd been Sam? Refusing to delve into that grim possibility, he headed for bed, knowing he had to work in the morning.

He and Lindsey only saw each other briefly the following morning, as she had to work and so did he. He couldn't get the conversation from the night before out of his mind, as he headed to the fire station.

"Hey, Monroe. How are you?" Jack Nelson, one of his fellow paramedics, greeted him when he walked in. "Did you have a good couple days off?"

"Yeah, did you?" Jack would have been surprised to know his time had been spent centered around nine-year-old kid, but he didn't bother to elaborate. A lot of the guys, especially the married ones with families, assumed he lived the wild, single guy lifestyle. And if he were honest, he'd earned that reputation. But that was in the past. The sad truth was that he hadn't been out with a woman in months.

Since Sam's death.

Since realizing how completely hung up he was on his best friend's widow.

"Have things been quiet?" He asked as they made their way into the kitchen. When they weren't fighting fires or responding to paramedic calls, they tended to eat.

Following his nose, he realized they were in for a treat. Big Joe Jansen was already cooking up a hearty breakfast feast.

"Pretty quiet. A few routine paramedic runs. No fire calls, though." Jack sounded disappointed.

Californians knew their sunny, warm and dry weather, predisposed them to fires. As much as a firefighter didn't want to see people suffer tragedies, there was something inside them that longed for the adrenaline rush of fighting a fire. It was one of the reasons he and Sam had applied to be a part of the smoke jumping crew. He liked knowing his talents were needed.

It had seemed like an adventure. Until he'd lost his best friend.

"Hungry?" Big Joe waved a spatula at them. "It's almost ready."

"I could eat." Austin dropped into a chair at the table. It was a good thing there was a weight room in the back, otherwise they'd grow fat and lazy from big Joe's cooking.

Although Lindsey's dinners were a pretty close second. He looked forward to going home after his twenty-four-hour long shifts knowing she was there.

Shying away from that dangerous thought, he listened as the guys argued over the latest sports games. They've just finished eating when their first call came in. Since Austin and Jack were the freshest of the bunch, they were identified as the first responders.

"What do we have?" Austin asked from the driver's seat.

"Sixty-four-year-old unconscious male with a history of heart problems," Jack repeated what the dispatcher had told him.

"He fell?"

"Not that we are aware of."

He pulled up in front of the patient's house. A woman he assumed was the gentleman's wife, waited anxiously for them in the doorway. "This way," she urged leading them through the house to the master bedroom.

Carrying his EMS pack and wheeling a gurney between them, Austin and Jack followed her. "What sort of heart problems does he have?" Austin asked.

"He had a heart attack about a year ago." The patient's wife pulled out a handwritten note as they entered the room, where the patient was still lying in bed. "These are the medications he's taking."

"Smart of you to write them down." He set the list aside and began a quick assessment, glad to note the patient was breathing, if barely. "Let's give him a little oxygen."

Jack turned on a portable tank and placed an oxygen mask over the patient's nose and mouth. The man groaned a little, indicating he wasn't as unconscious as Austin had originally thought. He connected the elderly man to their portable heart monitor and then obtained a blood pressure.

"BP low, 96 / 70, and he's in sinus tack with a rate of 142." Austin glanced at the medication list. "He takes a beta blocker, aspirin, and wears a nitroglycerin patch."

"We better get the patch off with his blood pressure so low." Jack opened the guy's shirt and removed it.

"Does he have any other medical problems?" Austin asked the hovering wife.

"He's diabetic but doesn't take any pills or insulin. He just watches his diet."

"Check a blood glucose level," Austin advised. The guy's vitals weren't great, but they were stable enough for transport. "I'll start an IV. "

"Sounds good." Jack pulled out the tiny glucometer and proceeded to prick the man's finger for a drop of blood while Austin inserted the antecubital intravenous catheter. While he worked, the wife explained how her husband had been sick with a cold for several days, staying in bed longer than normal period he didn't never bounced back.

After a few seconds the tiny machine beeped. "Wow, his glucose is critically high at 750," Jack announced.

"He must be in diabetic ketoacidosis," Austin said as he hung a bag of normal saline. During his paramedic career, he'd seen many patients in a similar condition. "We'll run fluids on the way to the hospital."

"You got it." With Jack's help they lifted the patient onto the gurney. The closest healthcare center was Sun Valley Community Hospital, so once they were situated in the ambulance, he radioed the dispatcher to relay a message about their impending arrival.

The staff in the emergency department were expecting them. He wasn't completely surprised to see Lindsey was the nurse waiting to take their patient. If he were honest, he'd admit he had been hoping to run into her there.

Either at work or at home, seeing Lindsey was the highlight of his day.

He rattled off the patient's vitals and glucose levels as they transferred him onto the cart.

"How much fluid did you give him?" Lindsay asked

with a frown.

"Only two-hundred cc's so far." He glanced at her trying to gauge why she was asking. "With this cardiac history, I didn't want to risk heart failure, but that is the treatment for DKA."

"I understand." She flashed a small smile. "But I don't smell any ketones on his breath so it makes me wonder if he really has DKA or something more serious like hyperosmolar, hyper glycemic non-ketotic coma."

He stared at her in surprise. That was something he'd never heard about. "What's the difference?"

"Profound dehydration causes HHNK, you said he's a diet controlled diabetic, right?" Austin nodded, impressed with her knowledge. "We'll know more as soon as we get some lab results back." She took the tube of blood she just drawn and handed it to a lab tech. "In HHNK, the patient usually has enough insulin in their body to prevent ketoacidosis, but not enough to allow the body to use the glucose appropriately. These patients are often much sicker than they look. HHNK is often misdiagnosed. And really, it's up to the doctor to make that call anyway."

On cue, a doctor walked into the room. "What do we have?"

Austin stood to the side, listening as Lindsey ran down the patient's history and current vitals. The guy's blood pressure had not improved, even after Jack removed the nitroglycerine patch.

"Run a twelve-lead EKG and then increase his fluids," Dr. Graff ordered. "Call me as soon as you get those lab results back."

"I will." Lindsey called the EKG tech over.

Austin knew there was no reason to stay other than his own personal need to know what exactly this guy's diagnosis was. He'd made an assumption about the DKA and it bothered him to think it may have been the wrong one. "Jack, let's hang out for a few minutes."

"No problem." Jack glanced around. "I wouldn't mind a cup of coffee, though."

"In the break room." Lindsey jerked her thumb over her shoulder in the general direction of the staff lounge.

Jack ambled off but Austin stayed right where he was. "How long does it take the chemistry results to come back?"

"Should be any minute now—they're usually pretty quick." She glanced at him. "What's wrong? You look worried."

He lifted his shoulder. "Maybe we should have treated him differently. The wife did say he hadn't been feeling well for a couple of days."

"Normally you wouldn't give a sixty-four-year-old a large influx of fluids, especially if he has a cardiac history," she assured him. "You did the right thing."

He appreciated her staunch support. This was exactly what he'd always admired about her. She never made the paramedic crew feel like second class citizens.

"Lindsey? Call from the lab on line three."

She picked up the nearest phone and he watched over her shoulder as she wrote down the various lab results. When she finished, she handed him the slip of paper. "Definitely HHNK. See? Ketones are negative."

He nodded handing the slip back. "So now what?"

She had already picked up the phone, placing a call to Dr. Graff. He listened as she relayed the information and then took more orders. She hung up the phone. "He's going to be admitted to the intensive care unit. They'll keep a close eye on him."

"Good." He tucked his hands in his pockets, reassured

that his and Jack's treatment hadn't been too far off the mark. "Thanks for letting me know."

"Any time." She turned her attention back to the patient and he glanced around for Jack. Was the guy still guzzling coffee in the lounge? He went back and found his partner. As they finished the rest of their newly computerized paperwork, he explained what Lindsey had taught him about their patient's illness.

"That's interesting," Jack agreed.

They headed toward the ambulance. Austin was about to slide into the driver's seat when he stopped, realizing he'd forgotten to tell Lindsey there was an extra Tai Kwon Do class that evening for Josh. As he was working, she would have to take him. Instead of calling her later, he decided to tell her now.

"Here." He tossed Jack the keys. "I'll be right back."

"Sure." Jack brightened at the chance to drive.

He went back inside, glancing around for Lindsey. Their patient was gone so she must have transported him up to the ICU already.

How long would that take? He glanced at his watch. Curious, he walked to the staff lounge, intending to ask one of Lindsey 's coworkers for an approximate timeframe. He was surprised to find Lindsey chatting with Mary, one of the other nurses.

"He's just a friend," Lindsey was saying. "You know his reputation around here as well as I do."

"Yeah, but people can change," Mary pointed out. "Maybe if you gave him a chance, he could be more than a friend."

"Austin? More than a friend? Never." Lindsey 's firm tone stopped him in his tracks just outside the doorway. "I could never be interested in a guy like him."

# CHAPTER SIX

Austin wished he could duck back out of the breakroom without being seen, but at that moment Mary, the nurse Lindsey had been talking to made eye contact.

Wasn't there some saying about people who eavesdropped never hearing good things about themselves? Yeah, so true.

Forcing himself to brazen it out he stepped further into the room. "Lindsey?" At the sound of his voice, she jumped around, her eyes wide and her cheeks flushed pink with embarrassment. "I forgot to mention, Josh has an extra Tai Kwon Do lesson tonight. You'll need to pick him up at four-thirty."

"Oh. Um... Okay. Thanks for letting me know." Her obvious distress tugged at his heart.

He flashed a reassuring smile, although her comment still stung. "No problem. Have a good day. See you tomorrow."

"You, too. Take care."

Leaving the staff lounge, he headed back out to where Jack was waiting in the ambulance. As his partner drove back to the firehouse, he replayed her comment in his mind. She could never be interested in a guy like him. Although he had vowed to stay away from her, the comment rankled. He shouldn't take it personally, he knew he had a bit of a reputation because he'd dated so many different women. The truth of the matter was that he'd never found the woman he was looking for. Maybe because he hadn't wanted to settle for anything less than what his parents had.

It wasn't until late into his shift that he realized Lindsey hadn't mentioned anything about avoiding relationships because she was still in love with Sam.

He knew she had to be grieving over losing her husband. He was nuts to even think about waiting around for the time she might get over Sam enough to start dating again.

But if that day ever came, would she consider giving him a chance?

He wasn't sure but decided it might be time to find out.

---

AFTER THAT MORTIFYING experience in the staff lounge, Lindsey was relieved she didn't have to face Austin until the next day. She couldn't believe he'd overheard her thoughtless comment. He did have a reputation with women, especially as he dated half the staff in the Sun Valley emergency department. But she shouldn't have been so harsh.

It had been the only way she could think of to get Mary's thoughts out of her head. Because she was attracted to him and had been surprised Mary had picked up on it.

Austin arrived home moments after Josh left for school

the next morning, yawning widely, his bloodshot eyes betraying his exhaustion.

"Bad night?" She glanced at him with sympathy.

"Busy night." He lifted a shoulder. "Nothing too horrible, just a lot of routine calls. Enough to keep us hopping all night, though. I don't think I slept even one hour."

"There's plenty of time now for you to get some sleep."

"I will." He glanced at her, as if just noticing her scrubs. "Are you working again today?"

She'd picked up an extra shift, desperate for some additional money. Especially as the bank had yet promised her a loan. "Yes. I'll be home by four o'clock. Call me if you need me to pick Josh up."

"I can do it." He hesitated, as if wanting to say something more. An awkward silence fell and it was on the tip of her tongue to apologize for being so blunt but then the moment passed as he bade her good night and headed down to his room.

She watched him disappear through the doorway, thinking that even after a long night he still looked as handsome as ever. What was wrong with her anyway? He wasn't the type of guy she should be attracted to. And not just because he dated a different woman every night.

Austin was a smoke jumper. A risk taker. An adrenaline junkie.

Even as she mentally compared him to Sam, she knew she wasn't being fair. Austin might like the thrill and excitement of being a smoke jumper, but he was very different from Sam.

Her husband had used smoke jumping as an excuse to avoid her. To avoid the family responsibilities he'd become to resent. Oh sure, he'd claimed it was only to make extra money, but then she'd discovered the full extent of his debt.

But what had bothered her the most was that Sam hadn't cared that his long absences only drove a deeper wedge between them.

As she headed to work, Lindsey thought back over those months before Sam had tested out to be a smoke jumper. If she were honest, she'd admit her marriage had been in trouble even then. Before Sam had begun to stay away from home for long periods of time. Maybe he had been partially right when he'd accused her of driving him away.

Maybe she had been more at fault for the disintegration of their marriage than she'd been willing to admit.

---

LINDSEY'S SHIFT STARTED SLOWLY, but soon patients were streaming in. When the EMT crew brought in a drunk driver who'd crashed his car into a street pole, she was reminded of her problems with Sam all over again.

Thankfully the patient, Jeff Jones, wasn't seriously injured. A gash across his forehead would need a few stitches, but otherwise Jeff was remarkably unhurt.

She shouldn't be surprised, considering Jeff's alcohol level was twice the legal limit. He'd admitted to having a couple of martinis over lunch. What had reminded her of Sam, though, had been when he'd claimed he was upset because his wife had announced she was leaving him.

Instantly she was back to the night before Sam had left for his smoke jumping mission. She'd told him she was filing for divorce. That when he returned from his mission, he should find somewhere else to stay. There had been a part of her that had thought he wouldn't care anyway as he'd spent more time away from her than at home.

But he had cared, or so he'd claimed. Then he'd died.

Uncomfortable with the memories, Lindsey concentrated on Jeff's minor injuries. She started an IV, infused plenty of fluids to help dilute the alcohol and even fed him a late lunch.

Toward the end of her shift Dr. Delaney cleared Jeff for discharge. She watched as the police took him away in handcuffs, arresting him for driving under the influence. Jeff had been totally dejected, telling her that for sure now his wife wouldn't give him a second chance.

If Sam had lived, would they have tried to make their marriage work? She had thought long and hard about even filing for divorce. She'd tried to talk to Sam, but he had no interest in seeing a counselor. And finally, their empty marriage had convinced her there was nothing to save. She knew there had to be more to a marriage, a partnership, then simple coexistence. It had hurt her deeply to know Sam preferred to be anywhere but at home.

Still, it wasn't as if Sam had been a bad guy. The truth was, they'd gotten married too young. Then they'd had gotten pregnant with Josh almost right away. The responsibility had been sobering. And somehow, over the years, the love between them had evaporated until there had been nothing left but dust.

She wished she had someone to talk to about her marriage. Someone who would understand her dilemma. Austin? She bit her lip uncertainly. Why not? Maybe it would be easier to view Austin as a friend if she started to treat him like one. Maybe once he knew what had really happened in her marriage, some of the attraction between them would fade. Love from afar was always easier than dealing with the reality of every day.

On her way home from work, Lindsey stopped by her house to pick up the mail. She had forgotten to go to the post office to temporarily change her mailing address to Austin's.

There were a few bills, but payment wasn't late as she'd arranged for electronic payments directly out of her checking account. It was one way to repair her crippled credit rating.

There was an envelope from Josh's school. Progress report? With a sense of dread she drove home, trying to prepare for the worst.

She knew Josh's grades had slipped over the past quarter. His poor grades, along with his truancy had been signs that she was losing him. In the week and a half they've been living with Austin, things had seemed better. Yet maybe that was wishful thinking? They'd only been here ten days. How much influence could Austin really have had in such a short time?

Entering Austin's house quietly so she wouldn't wake him up, she carried the mail into the kitchen. Taking a deep breath, she opened the envelope and read Josh's progress report.

A heavy weight rolled off her chest. A couple of C's but more B's and even one A-, something she'd never seen on his report card. Much better than the last progress report she'd received.

She was grinning like an idiot when Austin walked into the kitchen, wearing a T-shirt and a pair of athletic shorts, his hair damp from a recent shower. He was up earlier than she'd expected as Josh didn't need to be picked up for another twenty minutes.

"Good news?" He asked, opening the fridge and pouring a large glass of orange juice.

"Very good news." She waved the progress report at him. "Josh is doing better in school."

"Really?" Austin's eyes gleamed with interest as he reached for the report, shutting the fridge door with his elbow as he scanned it with a quick eye. "Wow this is great. I'm glad."

"Me, too." She knew much of this was because of Austin. "You were right. Temporarily moving in with you and starting him in Tai Kwon Do classes has made a huge difference. I don't know how to thank you."

"You don't have to thank me," he protested. His compelling green gaze met hers. "I care about you and Josh. I'm happy to help."

She knew he meant it. If only Sam had felt the same way. At least before their marriage had crumbled. Ridiculous tears threatened, and she changed the subject to prevent from getting maudlin. "Maybe we should go out to dinner tonight to celebrate."

"I like that idea." He offered a lopsided smile. "But do we have to let Josh pick the place? We're likely to end up at some pizza joint if we do."

She had to laugh at his rueful expression. "I know. But they are his grades after all."

"I guess you're right." He stared at her and suddenly the kitchen seemed too small. Or maybe it was just the memory of their kiss that made her hyper aware of him.

"Well." She cleared her throat to cover the awkward moment. "If you're sure you're up to a night out, I'll pick up Josh and meet you back here."

"I can pick up Josh," he quickly offered. "You just walked in the door from work. Why don't you relax? Josh may have some homework to finish first anyway before we're ready to go."

His consideration was so novel, so nice, she couldn't refuse. "All right. Thanks."

"I'll see if I can talk Josh out of a pizza place on the way home," he added with a quick grin.

"Good luck with that." She laughed as he left, thinking how odd it was that Austin, the guy who had never been married or had children of his own, managed to share the parenting duties more fairly than her husband ever had.

A trait that made him twice as attractive.

———

AUSTIN HAD NOT BEEN able to talk Josh out of a pizza celebration, but he did agree to Josh's request to bring Tony along for dinner.

He'd wanted to take Lindsey to a nice restaurant for a change. Instead, they were destined to eat at popular pizza place with a small arcade attached.

When he saw Lindsey in the kitchen wearing a gauzy skirt that swept her ankles, with a matching spaghetti strap camisole tap, he fought a surge of desire.

She was so beautiful. Alluring, without even trying.

Okay, then. Maybe it was a good thing they were going to a noisy pizza place. Anything more intimate and he might make a total fool out of himself.

The need to kiss Lindsey, to hold her close would not leave him alone. He wanted her more than ever. Despite overhearing her comment about his reputation, he still longed to hold her. And kiss her.

Would she look at him differently if she knew his playboy days were over? Would she be willing to give him a chance if she knew how much he cared for her?

How he was falling in love with her?

Thirty minutes later, after both boys had finished their homework, they headed out. Josh and Tony kept up a steady stream of conversation in the back seat as he drove to the restaurant. Once inside, they placed their order for large pizzas loaded with everything Josh and Tony liked to eat. Then the boys disappeared into the arcade, leaving him and Lindsey alone.

"How was your day?" He asked when the boys had left.

She shrugged. "Mostly uneventful, although one of my patients was a drunk driver who crashed into a streetlight."

He levered his brow. "Drinking at noon?"

Her smile was strained. "Yeah, well, it seems he was trying to drown his sorrows as his wife had just announced she was leaving him."

"I see." Her pensive gaze tugged at him. Something about this patient seemed to have gotten to her.

"Austin, have you given up smoke jumping?"

Her abrupt question surprised him. He sipped his soft drink, trying to figure out how to answer her. "I'm not sure. I went back right after our—ah, argument, but all I could think about was how Sam had died. I went back too soon." He lifted a shoulder and grimaced. "To be honest, I don't know if I'll ever be ready to go back."

She frowned, drawing imaginary patterns on the table with her fingertip. "It was my fault, you know."

Was she talking about Sam's death? "What? Lindsey how could you possibly be at fault? You were hundreds of miles away when he died." Austin knew he was the one who'd caused Sam's death. Not her.

She stared at the tabletop, her voice so quiet he had to strain to hear. "I'm sure Sam mentioned we were having a few—problems."

"No, actually, he didn't." He frowned. Why hadn't Sam mentioned their problems? Maybe because, like most guys, talking about all that personal stuff wasn't easy. He tried to reassure her. "Hey, most marriages have their ups and downs. I'm sure your problems were similar to those in many other marriages."

She sat back, rubbing her hands over her arms as if she were cold and slowly shook her head. "No. They were far more serious than that."

Serious? He didn't know what to say. Sam had never breathed a word about any of this. Then a coldness swept over him. "What happened? Did he do something to you? Hurt you in some way?" The idea of Sam lifting a hand to his wife and to his son filled him with anger.

"No, he never hurt us, not physically." Her expression turned even more grim. "Sam spent so much time away from home it seemed there was nothing left. No marriage. No companionship. Nothing."

He blew out a breath, realizing what she was saying. The competition to become a smoke jumper was fierce. Only the best of the best made the crew. He and Sam had both been honored to be chosen. But the lengthy stints away from home, up to three months at a time, could create havoc on a relationship. And suddenly he was upset with Sam. What had his buddy been thinking, to put a stupid job ahead of his wife and son?

He across the table, capturing her small hands in his. "I understand. It's not your fault."

"No, you don't understand." She tried to tug her hands from his. "Don't you see? His death was really my fault. I filed for divorce, right before you guys were called up for that fire. I filed for divorce and told Sam he needed to move out." Her gaze clung to his. "And that's why he died that day."

# CHAPTER SEVEN

Austin tightened his grip on her hands and leaned forward, his gaze intense. "Listen, there's something you need to know..."

Josh and Tony came running back to their table before he could explain what had really happened the night Sam had died. The details he should have told her a long time ago.

"Mom! Tony and I each won a game. Do you have more quarters? We need to stay long enough for a tiebreaker! Otherwise, how will we know who won?"

Lindsey gave another subtle tug on her hands and this time he reluctantly let her go. She appeared flustered as she ran her fingers through her blonde hair. "Maybe later, right now I think they're bringing our pizzas."

Sure enough, their server approached their table with two large pizzas and several soft drinks on her tray. She set everything down on the table, the kids barely waiting for her to move out of the way before digging eagerly into the food. Josh seemed happy, considering the way his mouth was stuffed with gooey cheese, pepperoni, and tangy pizza sauce.

He didn't mind when the rest of the evening centered around Josh, but he kept hearing Lindsey's words echoing in his brain.

She'd been planning to divorce Sam. Had asked Sam to move out of the house. The night he'd kissed her in his kitchen, she couldn't have been pretending he was Sam if she'd been planning to divorce him.

Could she?

Probably not. Yet she'd clearly told her nurse colleague that there was no way she could ever be interested in him as more than a friend.

Because of his reputation of dating many women.

He watched as she laughed at some story Josh was telling, the lyrical sound washing over him. She called to his senses the way no woman ever had. He'd always admired her, and now she was available. More so than he'd realized.

If he could convince her he'd given up his old ways, maybe he'd stand a chance.

He could face anything life threw at him, with Lindsey by his side.

LINDSEY COULDN'T BELIEVE she'd bared her soul to Austin about her plans to divorce Sam.

A secret she'd been carrying for months.

Austin bantered with Josh and Tony teasing them about their video games and their Tai Kwon Do lessons. The boys seemed to enjoy having his undivided attention. Telling Austin the truth about her relationship with Sam had been cathartic. At least, now he knew that while she grieved Sam's death, it wasn't the same grief she'd have felt if she still loved him.

The sad truth was that her love for Sam had died a long time ago.

And why it was so important for Austin to know that was something she didn't want to examine too closely.

After dinner, she watched with a mother's indulgence as the boys and Austin played one last tiebreaker video game, before they headed home. They dropped Tony off at his house along the way.

At Austin's, Josh scrambled to get ready for bed. To keep busy, she folded a load of towels she'd tossed in the dryer, listening as Austin spoke with her son.

"I'm really proud of the way you've improved your grades and the way you've been staying in school," she heard Austin say. "Keep up the good work, okay?"

"I will. Now that Tony and I are doing Tai Kwon Do, school doesn't seem so bad."

"Maybe it helps to think about something besides losing your dad, huh?" She glanced over in time to see Austin give Josh's shoulder a gentle squeeze.

"Yeah. I still miss him, but I don't think about it all the time anymore," Josh agreed.

She paused in the middle of folding the last towel. She hadn't realized Josh had skipped school mostly because of missing his dad. Her heart ached for her son and she wished there was something more she could do for him.

But grief needed to run its course. Between Austin and their counseling sessions, Josh would continue to learn to deal with the loss of his father.

She finished folding the last towel then came out of the

laundry room to join Josh and Austin. She glanced at her son. "All set? Did you brush your teeth?"

"Yep. See?" He bared his teeth for her and then turned to Austin. "Good night, Austin."

"Good night, Josh." Austin stepped out of the room and she waited until her son crawled into bed before sitting on the edge of the mattress. "I'm proud of you for staying in school too, you know."

"I know." Thankfully, he wasn't too old that he didn't mind reaching up to give her a hug. "It's not so bad. I guess I don't hate school as much as I used to."

Maybe the worst of his grief was fading. She hoped so, for his sake. "I'm glad. And I'm always here if you want to talk." She returned his hug and pressed a kiss to his forehead, wishing she could ease his pain in some way. He was growing up so fast. "Goodnight."

"G'night." He yawned and she laughed softly, crossing the room to turn out the light and then closing the door behind her.

It was only nine o'clock and as she wasn't quite ready to go to bed, she wandered down the hall looking for Austin. He wasn't in the kitchen or in the living room, watching TV. The patio doors in the living room were open, leading to the enclosed backyard. She found him sitting outside in a lounge chair wearing a T-shirt and swim trunks, using his toe to make waves in the calm water of his pool.

"I'm sure you'll have trouble sleeping tonight." She came out to stand beside him. "It's hard to get back on a normal schedule after pulling an all nighter."

"Maybe a little," he admitted. He gestured to the empty lounge chair beside him. "Have a seat. I was just thinking of going for a swim. Care to join me?"

A swim with Austin sounded like heaven. The cool water looked as if it would soothe her ragged nerves. Yet she knew that accepting Austin's offer would not be the smartest thing in the world.

She liked him far too much already. More so after everything he'd done for her son.

"I don't know." She hesitated, trying to think of a good excuse. Difficult to come up with something when she really wanted to join him.

"Please? The water is refreshing." He stood, stripped off his T-shirt and jumped into the water making a huge splash and raining drops of water on her heated skin. Sluicing water off his face, he tossed back his wet hair and grinned. "Swimming alone isn't much fun. Come on in. The water is awesome."

She wavered, torn between what she wanted and what was smart. Thinking back to their kiss in the kitchen, she remembered how mortified she'd been to know he'd pulled away from her. Was that because he was only interested in having fun? He had a reputation for avoiding serious relationships. At the time she assumed he'd pulled away because she wasn't his type.

Yet things had changed since then. They were friends. Two friends could hang out together without getting all weird about it. "All right. I'll change into my swimsuit."

She hurried and dug through her dresser until she found her swimsuit. It was a modest royal blue one piece that matched her eyes. Although when she walked back outside, she felt extremely self-conscious wearing the figure hugging nylon. Austin was doing laps lengthwise in the pool, so she stood at the edge and dipped her toe in, testing the water temperature.

Cool, but not unbearably so. Refreshing in the muggy heat of the night. Before she could lower herself to the edge, a hand grabbed her foot and jerked her off balance.

"Yikes!" She squeaked before plummeting into the cool depths of the pool.

When she emerged, spitting mad, she heard Austin's deep chuckle. The sound soothed her annoyance. She hadn't heard him laugh much lately. "You'd better watch out," she threatened. "I don't get mad, I get even."

"Oh yeah?" He taunted. "Give it your best shot, Babe."

Babe? She wasn't anyone's *babe*. Betting that Austin didn't know she'd spent several summers on the beach as a lifeguard, she slid beneath the water and silently made her way across the pool. When she found his legs treading water, she gave a hard yank and then jackknifed out of reach.

They goofed around in the water, each trying to sneak up and dunk the other. Austin was fast, but she had stealth, keeping the score fairly even until he caught her off guard for a second dunking moments after the first.

She pushed off the bottom of the pool breaking the surface while coughing and sputtering, having swallowed a mouthful of water.

His strong arms lifted her up, holding her safely against his chest while she struggled to breathe.

"I'm sorry, are you all right?" His tone was contrite.

She gasped between coughs. "I give up. You win." She rested her hands on his slick broad shoulders to help maintain her balance.

"I'm sorry," he repeated in a low tone. His chest was warm, her legs entwining with his as he held her. "I shouldn't have let things get so competitive. Blame it on growing up with five siblings. My older brothers were always trying to get the better of me."

"I'm okay," she managed, although she wasn't certain that was true. Being close to him was wreaking havoc with her common sense. The way he held her so tenderly in his arms, she knew she'd better move away before she did something she'd regret.

Although she honestly couldn't say she'd regretted kissing him the other night.

His arms tightened, pulling her close. "Lindsey," he murmured, smoothing her wet hair away from her face before lowering his head toward her mouth. She met him halfway, eager to taste him.

How was it possible this kiss was better than the first? There wasn't any hesitation between them. The moment their mouths touched, she parted her lips, inviting him deeper.

She barely noticed when he drew her toward the shallow end of the pool. When their legs bumped against the steps, she broke free.

"Austin?" She wasn't sure what she was asking.

"Come here, to the lounge chair." His voice was low and husky. "We need to talk."

"Talk?" She blinked, trying to read his expression in the darkness. Since when did a man stop kissing a woman in order to talk?

A low chuckle escaped him and he stretched out on the lounger pulling her down beside him. There was barely room for the both of them. "Lindsey, I think it's obvious how much I want you. But I promised you could stay here without strings. This wasn't part of our deal."

He was sweet, the way he spoke so earnestly. "I know."

She wasn't sure what else to say. She rested against him for a moment, cherishing his closeness.

"I guess what I'm saying is that I don't want to give you a reason to leave," he admitted. "I would never want you to feel uncomfortable."

His concern touched her heart. She'd never wanted a man as much as she wanted Austin. True passion had been missing from her life for what seemed like forever. It was difficult to walk away from it now. She angled up to look into his eyes. "Maybe I'm looking for a reason to stay."

"I'd like that." Then hastily added, "I mean, that you stay. Not that I pressure you for anything more."

She rested the palm of her hand on his damp chest, trying to put her feelings into words. But before she could gather her scattered thoughts, she heard the screen door open.

"Mom? My tummy hurts."

They froze at the sound of Josh's voice. She scrambled off the lounge nearly falling flat on her face. "I'm coming, Josh," she said loudly. Then in a whisper she added, "Likely too much pizza. I'm sorry."

"No need to apologize. I understand," he assured her.

She headed inside to Josh, both glad and sad to have their kiss interrupted.

What was she thinking, playing with fire? She was lucky Josh had interrupted when he had before she managed to get burned.

JOSH FINALLY FELL ASLEEP, after she'd given him some anti gas pills she'd found in Austin's medicine cabinet.

By the next morning, Josh was tired but otherwise felt fine and insisted on going to school.

She'd been tempted to keep him at home, but had decided against it, knowing her son had already missed more than enough school. The biggest problem was that she and Austin both had the day off.

And she couldn't help reliving their heated kiss at the side of his pool.

Was he planning to pick up where they'd left off?

Did she want him to?

Months ago, she'd accused him of trying to take over her life. And while that was sort of true, the real reason she'd pushed him away had been because she'd known it would be like this between them. Hot. Sensual. Intense. Far too tempting.

She needed to get a grip. After dropping Josh off at school, she didn't go back to Austin's. Instead, she'd decided to go to the bank to check on the status of her loan.

The loan officer kept her waiting almost twenty minutes. When he finally returned, she could tell by the serious expression on his face that the news wasn't promising.

"I'm sorry, Mrs. Winters, but as a high-risk borrower, you don't qualify for a loan."

Stunned, she stared at him. "How is that possible? I have the house as collateral. And I need to pay for the repairs from the fire."

"Yes, but the house is in need of repairs, and unfortunately your credit rating is, well..." he shrugged. "I'm sorry."

"Sorry?" She glared at him. "What do you suggest I do?"

He shifted uncomfortably in his chair, tugging at his tie. "There are places that will give high risk loans to people in your situation for a much higher interest rate. You may want to try for one of those."

Annoyed, she grabbed her purse and stood. "Thanks for nothing." She turned and walked out of the bank, her cheeks burning with embarrassment. A high interest loan because she was high risk. The payments were going to be difficult enough, without adding a high interest rate to the mix.

Depressed, she headed over to her house to check on the status of the repairs. Stepping inside, she was glad to see there was some evidence of work that had been done to date. There were bits of wiring scattered around the floor, along with the fine sheen of drywall dust, yet the place was empty.

Where were the construction workers? Was it a holiday of some sort? It was the middle of spring, it couldn't possibly be Columbus Day. Or President's day. She frowned. Memorial Day was at least six weeks away.

As she turned to leave Austin stepped through the doorway, surprised to find her there. "What is it? What's wrong?" He looked concerned at seeing the frustration on her face.

"Where is everyone? Why aren't they working?"

"The crew is working on a couple of projects at the same time," he explained. "There's a lot of building going on in the area and besides, it's one of the reasons their bid was lower. I knew it was going to take a little longer this way."

"I thought you were going to put a rush on this," she shot back, knowing she sounded angry but unable to help herself.

He looked confused. "I tried Lindsey, but you were also concerned about the cost so I thought cheaper was better."

She let out her breath in a deep, heavy sigh. She was

being unreasonable. How could she argue if it was cheaper? Even the less expensive rates were going to be difficult for her to pay. Especially without a bank loan.

"Let me show you around." Austin pointed out what the electricians were doing, going into a technical explanation of how they were going to bring the wiring up to code. Then he described the repairs needed to remove the water damaged drywall, extending over half of the corner of her house. The more he talked, the more depressed she became.

It would take weeks to get everything completed. If she were lucky.

She forced herself to meet Austin's gaze. "I was turned down for a bank loan. I'm going to look into other options, but I thought you should know. Don't worry, I'll figure out some way to pay you back."

"It's no problem," he quickly assured her. "Please don't even worry about paying me back. Not now. Just make sure you and Josh have what you need."

A flash of anger burned in her belly. Did he expect her to borrow money from him? Then conveniently forget to pay him back? What sort of person did he think she was? "If it takes longer for me to get a loan approved, I'll pay the going interest rate, in addition to the balance and the amount you've paid out so far."

He scowled. "Don't be ridiculous. I'm not going to take money for helping you. Forget about paying any interest. I told you, don't worry about repaying me back."

"No. I won't forget about the interest or the money." She crossed her arms over her chest. "I know you sincerely care about my welfare, and Josh's too. But you're acting as if I can't support myself." Memories of her mother moving her from place to place came rushing back. Lindsey had considered asking him for a loan, but not anymore. As much as she hated to admit it, the high interest place would probably be a better way to go.

Especially considering the heated kisses they'd exchanged beneath the stars last night.

"There is another way to do this," he said in a low tone.

"Oh yeah?" Warily she looked at him. "How?"

"You could marry me and move in with me permanently."

# CHAPTER EIGHT

Austin hadn't planned to propose, but the moment the words left his mouth he realized marrying Lindsey was the perfect solution.

Too bad Lindsey's reaction was the opposite of encouraging.

She went pale, her eyes wide and her pupils dilated to the point he couldn't see the blue of her irises. She shook her head, taking several steps backward as if needing to get away from him.

"Marry you? Are you kidding?" Her voice rose, nearly hysterical. "No. Oh, no. Absolutely not."

He tried not to be hurt by her emphatic refusal. His fault, for blurting out the proposal without any forewarning. And really, couldn't he have chosen a more romantic setting? But she didn't have to act as if being with him was akin to having hot needles stuck in her eyes. Why was marrying him completely out of the question? Their relationship had gone from mere friendship to a heck of a lot more on the patio surrounding his pool last night.

Even she couldn't deny the attraction simmering

between them. The desire that had washed over them during that amazing kiss. He cared about her and this was his way of proving he wasn't interested in a fling or a temporary liaison.

He wanted far more.

"Lindsey, I know I shouldn't have blurted it out like that, but I want you to know I'm serious. I—we don't have to do anything right away. Just think about it, okay?" He took a step toward her.

"No!" She spun on her heel and ran from the house. He was so shocked, it took him a moment to follow. She was surprisingly quick, jumping into her car and backing out of the driveway before he could blink. She drove down Puckett Street, as if a pack of wolves were snapping at her heels.

He stared after her bright yellow car, watching as the taillights disappeared around the corner.

Sighing heavily, he massaged the muscles behind his neck.

He was an idiot. His impatience had caused him to blow it with Lindsey, big time.

---

LINDSEY WAS SO upset her hands were shaking. She couldn't believe Austin had proposed marriage! Out of pity! To help her get out of debt!

Worse, she'd almost said yes. Had been far too tempted to say yes.

What was wrong with her? This was her fault. She was sending conflicting signals to Austin, playing in the pool with him one minute, arguing over her house repairs the next. Kissing him as if she were desperate and starved for love and attention. No wonder he'd proposed. Was she more like her mother than she realized?

She shivered at the thought. She needed to move out of Austin's house as soon as possible.

She managed to calm down enough to drive to the closest high interest brokerage house. They were more than happy to lend her money in exchange for an astronomical interest rate. She stared at the numbers of what her monthly payments would be and tried not to show her alarm. One extra shift a pay period couldn't be enough. She'd have to work two extra shifts in order to make ends meet.

Yet, what choice did she have? She didn't want Austin to think she'd marry him to avoid paying her debts. And the project needed to be done. Without giving herself time to talk herself out of it, she signed the papers and walked away with a fat check and the heavy responsibility of high interest loan payments.

At Austin's house, she set the check in the center of the kitchen table, where he couldn't help but see it when he came home. She told herself it was better this way.

He wasn't her type. She knew full well his reputation wasn't exaggerated. Many nurses in the emergency department had raved over what it had been like to go out with him. His proposal had caught her so off guard, she didn't know what to do or to say.

Avoiding him wouldn't be easy, not while they were living together in one house. Where could she go if she and Josh did need to move out? She couldn't afford a hotel, not with the new loan payments. She had friends from work, but none of them had much extra room. She sat on the edge of the bed in the guest bedroom and gazed around helplessly.

She was stuck here until she could find another place to stay.

———

AUSTIN KNEW how much he'd blown it with Lindsey when she avoided him for the rest of the day. He saw the check on the kitchen table from one of those high interest loan places but refused to take it. Paying inflated interest rates wouldn't help her become independent. She was already independent, doing a fine job of raising her son on her own. Why couldn't she see that?

He paced the length of his home, trying to relax his tense muscles. He shouldn't have shocked her with his proposal. Even though he'd meant every word. The idea of marrying Lindsey didn't scare him as much as it probably should. In truth, he'd never planned on marrying anyone. There wasn't a woman he'd dated with whom he'd wanted to spend the rest of his life.

And despite his tendency to avoid deep relationships, he didn't take marriage lightly. Thanks to the example set by his parents, he believed in marrying for keeps. That was the main reason he'd been so picky before.

Giving Lindsey the space she needed wasn't easy. He missed her. He missed talking to her even if it was just to hear about her day. Or to tell her about his.

He was almost grateful he was scheduled to work the following day. Living in the same house with her when she was barely speaking to him was difficult. At least Josh was talking to him or things would have gotten extremely uncomfortable.

He left the house the following morning before he even saw Lindsey. He received his first call within the hour, responding to a bad single vehicle crash on the interstate. After hitting a concrete barrier, the vehicle had flipped over and skidded on its hood for nearly fifty feet.

He was glad to be partnered with Big Joe to assist with the extrication. Two teams had been dispatched to the scene of the crash and traffic was backed up for miles. Luckily, both occupants of the car, a husband and his wife, had been wearing their seat belts or the outcome would have been deadly.

"Are you both okay?" He knelt on the ground to peer into the space where the driver side window had once been. The driver looked to be worse off than his female passenger.

"My chest hurts."

Austin didn't like the way the guy looked—he was pale, sweaty and complaining of chest pain. Had he suffered a heart attack before the crash or as a result of the air bag deployment while flipping over the concrete barrier and sliding on the car's roof?

"Let's get some oxygen on you." He reached in to wrap the oxygen mask around the guy's head. "On a scale of one to ten with ten being the worst pain you've ever felt, how much does your chest hurt?"

"Eight. Maybe a nine." The man's words were muffled by the oxygen mask.

"Let's try some nitroglycerin." Big joe pulled out a small vial of the soluble tablets.

He urged the patient to place the medication under his tongue. While they gave the nitro a chance to work, he and Big Joe discussed the best way to get the two victims out of the car.

"Through the window," Big Joe decided. "It will be tight, though." He gave a yank on the door, but it wouldn't budge. "Unless we want to wait for the jaws of life to get here?"

"No, let's try the window. I'll cut through his seat belt." Austin used his knife to free the driver and then slowly eased the man out of the car, doing his best to keep his patients head and neck in alignment.

"How's your pain?" He asked when the driver was free.

"A little better." The driver lifted bloody hands to his chest, rubbing the center. "Still hurts, though."

Joe let's start an IV and give him some morphine. Austin didn't like the driver's pale, cold, clammy skin. They needed to get his pain under control, and quickly.

With big Joe's help they managed to get the driver safely strapped onto the longboard and then up and onto the gurney. Using the padded head and shoulder blocks, he kept the guy's neck stabilized as Joe started the IV.

The driver relaxed once they had the morphine in him. But hooking him up to their portable monitored showed he had some acute myocardial changes in his heart. Austin quickly called the hospital and discussed the case with the emergency doctor as they prepared to transport him for further treatment. The second team that had arrived, took control of their patients' wife. Thankfully she didn't look as badly hurt.

An emergency department doctor met them at the doorway of the ambulance bay. He shouldn't have been disappointed not to see Lindsey. He and Joe wheeled the patient inside. The doctor had already contacted the cardiologist on duty and they had discussed the need for the patient to go straight to the cardiac cath lab. He and Joe assisted with transporting the patient to the third-floor cardiac care area.

He was glad they'd been able to get the poor guy out of

his car without taking too much time. From the concerned looks on the nursing staff's faces, it appeared time was of the essence.

When he and Joe returned to the emergency department, he saw Lindsey across the room taking care of the passenger of the motor vehicle crash. As much as he wanted to talk to her, now wasn't the time. She saw him, though, and acknowledged him with a nod and a smile.

His heart lifted. Had she gotten over being mad at him? Maybe she wasn't the type to hold a grudge for long. Too bad they didn't have time to talk. But maybe tomorrow, after his twenty-four-hour shift was over, there would be time to make amends.

The rest of his day remained busy. He'd thought about calling Lindsey at least a dozen times but managed to talk himself out of it. He knew it was better to have their next conversation in person, rather than over the phone. He wanted to be able to read her expression, there had already been enough miscommunication between them.

That night, as he stared up at the ceiling over his bunk in the fire station, he relived those moments at the pool. The fun they'd had playing in the water, and then the kiss that had morphed into instant explosive desire.

He was dreaming of Lindsey when the fire bells went off. The alarm had him jumping out of bed and sliding down the fire pole before he was fully awake. He stepped into his gear, drew it on and was seated in the fire truck in less than two minutes. He wished there had been time for coffee to help clear the cobwebs of sleep from his mind, but no such luck.

"Three alarm blaze in an apartment building on Hickory Ave," Big Joe informed him.

He nodded indicating he understood. Their siren

wailed as they flew through the streets. Apartment building fires were not good—too many potential victims.

The ride to the blaze didn't take long as there was very little traffic at four-thirty in the morning. He jumped out of the truck, taking the point position of going in first.

He was somewhat relieved to see there were almost a dozen people huddled together outside. Maybe they all had smoke detectors.

The fire chief was on scene, giving orders. "There's a family of five unaccounted for in apartment number 318, and an elderly couple in unit number 314 located on either side of the burning unit. We suspect the fire has already begun to spread into the roof. Monroe, you and Joe going after the family of five—there's a five-year old boy and a six-year old girl. The youngest child is just an infant. Hanks and Bishop, take the elderly couple. I have more responders on the way if you need help. Let's go!"

He didn't need to be told twice. The thought of kids being trapped in a burning apartment was horrifying. He took a moment to send up a prayer that God would watch over them before he took the stairs up to the third-floor apartment.

Smoke thicker than pea soup hung in the hallway when he reached the tap. Keeping his breathing even through the face mask he made his way down the hall to the apartment housing the family of five. He tested the door with his gloved hand, gauging the level of warmth before kicking it in.

The smoke was slightly less inside, but he wasn't reassured by that. Especially if the roof of the building was already compromised.

He and Joe searched the main apartment for victims before making their way down the hall to the bedrooms.

They found the kid's bedroom first, but there was only one child in bed, the little girl. The other bed was empty. He motioned for Big Joe to grab the six-year-old while he continued making his way down to the second bedroom. The parents were there, with a small infant in a cradle at the foot of the bed.

He couldn't believe they were all sleeping despite the thick smoke. If they had smoke alarms, they obviously weren't working. He picked up the baby and then woke the parents. The couple moved slowly, as if they were drugged. The smoke had already robbed their brains of oxygen. Ignoring them for the moment, he ran with the infant outside, using his radio to let the ground crew know they'd found survivors.

After handing the kids over to the paramedic crew he and Joe hurried back inside to assist the parents. And where was the third child? The parents were having trouble walking under their own power, so he and Big Joe carried them down the stairs to the fresh air outside.

"We lost the roof. I need every firefighter to get out of the building—now!" His Fire Chief shouted.

"We're missing a child," Austin said. "I need to go back in."

His boss glanced up at the building where flames could be seen shooting from the roof. "It's too dangerous."

"I'll be quick. He's only five." Austin turned and ran back inside before his boss could order him to stand down. He knew the kid was in there somewhere. Hiding under the bed? Or maybe in the bathroom? He didn't know for sure but he wouldn't rest until he'd found him.

He checked the bathroom first, but it was empty. Searching the kid's bedroom next, he crawled on the floor, peering under the bed. Sure enough, he saw the small shape of a child curled in the corner furthest from the edge of the bed.

"Come on, we need to get outside." He reached his arm under the bed, groping for the boy. When he touched the child's arm, the kid screamed.

He snatched his arm back. What in the world? Was the boy hurt? He didn't want to make things worse, so he stood, grabbed the headboard and tipped the entire frame up on its end so he could see the child.

The little boy was coughing and crying hysterically, but there were no other signs of injury. Lifting his face mask off, he placed it on the young boy for a few minutes. He knew it was protocol to keep his mask on at all times, but the way the kid was coughing and crying, and the boy needed oxygen more than he did.

"Come on, buddy, we need to get you out of here." He placed his face mask back on, picked the child up and made his way back to the hallway. He'd reached the living room, when a loud crack echoed through the room and parts of the ceiling came crashing down on his head.

Pressing the child's head to his chest, he hunched his shoulders, protecting the boy as best he could as he continued pushing toward the door. The entire apartment was on fire now, and he knew they didn't have much time. Debris from the ceiling hit him on the back, and he stumbled to his knees, barely hanging on to the child with one arm as he used the other to brace himself from falling on his face.

Just when Austin was beginning to fear he wouldn't make it out of there after all, Big Joe loomed in the doorway. "Monroe?"

"Here." Giving a last gigantic push, he stood and stumbled toward his partner. For a moment Sam's face swam before him. He blinked and saw Big Joe, who hauled him and the little boy toward the stairwell.

"Your back is smoking. What happened?" Big Joe asked as they stepped over debris lying on the floor.

He couldn't answer but followed Big Joe down the stairs and all the way outside. He was surprised to discover the sun was already up. He must have been inside the building longer than he'd thought.

The paramedic crew surrounded him, taking the boy from his arms and then pulling off his gear. He tried to tell them he was fine, but his voice came out as a weak croak.

They slapped oxygen on his face and hustled him over to the waiting ambulance. They continued plucking at his clothes and he yelped in pain when they found the spot in the center of his back that felt like hot lava.

One of them slapped a cold wet towel over the spot which helped a little. "Get him to the hospital, STAT!"

"I'm fine." His voice was still husky, and he was more worried about the little boy than himself. He tried to get off the stretcher, but strong hands held him down. He gave up, deciding to put his faith in God.

Disconcerting to be the patient when he was normally stationed on the other side of the bed. Visions of the wildfire he'd fought alongside Sam danced at the edge of his mind. He must have blacked out for a few minutes because suddenly he was in the brightly lit emergency department with faces leaning over him.

Lindsey's face? His gaze clung to her familiar features as he tried to reassure her that he was fine. The frank concern in her eyes and the seriousness of her expression betrayed the depth of her worry.

As they gave him medication to help with the pain, his last conscious thought was regret that he'd put that expression of fear in her eyes. He should have remembered he wasn't only responsible for himself.

He was responsible for Lindsey and Josh, too. He needed to take better care of himself, for their sake.

---

LINDSEY COULDN'T BELIEVE it when the ambulance crew wheeled Austin in as her next patient. The entire emergency department was swamped with other victims from the fire, thankfully most weren't badly injured.

She'd learned Austin saved a young boy's life.

Almost at the expense of his own.

As she helped care for Austin, she was relieved to note his injuries weren't life threatening. His lungs didn't sound the greatest, and the emergency department physician ordered him to stay on thirty percent oxygen via face mask until his pulse ox readings crept up to the ninety percent range. He could have been so much worse.

"Lindsey?"

She turned from the computer to see Austin had finally woken up. The morphine they'd given him had put him under for almost thirty minutes. Thankfully, his vital signs remained stable. "I'm here." She took his hand in hers, giving him a reassuring squeeze. "How are you feeling?"

"Better." His voice was low and husky and would have been sexy if she hadn't been worried about his vocal cords swelling from the smoke damage. "Water?"

"Sure." She helped him sit up, keeping well away from the small burned area and held the cup for him as he drank. Seeing how helpless he looked shook her more than she cared to admit.

"The boy? Do you know how the young boy is doing?"

She knew he meant Noah Peterson, the boy who'd been taken by chopper to the Children's Hospital in Los Angeles. She nodded. "They flew him to Childrens for closer observation."

He looked worried. "Childrens?"

"Yes. His breathing wasn't very good. They were talking about possibly using hyperbaric treatments on him, which we don't have here."

He frowned. "Poor kid was in the apartment too long. We couldn't find him. He was hiding under the bed."

She put a soothing hand on his forearm. "It's not your fault. You saved his life by finding him when you did."

"I pray I found him in time."

"You did." She squeezed his arm. "Try to rest now, okay?"

His crooked smile was sheepish. "I guess I'm not used to being the patient."

"No kidding," she responded in a dry tone. He was always so strong, invincible. It was only because of God's grace that his injuries weren't worse.

"I'm sorry," he whispered, his eyes half closed with fatigue. "I shouldn't have proposed... stupid..."

She stared at him, holding her breath. Now he thought it was stupid to want to marry her? It hurt to hear that. Although maybe he was specifically referring to his plan to marry her only to keep her out of debt. If he thought that was stupid, she had to agree. Marriage should be about love and commitment, not a free ride.

A lesson her mother hadn't learned.

Besides, she wasn't that broke that she needed to accept a pity proposal. She would be fine. She'd make the high monthly payments by working an extra shift every week. Everything would be okay.

She had no choice but to make it work.

---

THEY KEPT Austin for observation for a couple of hours. The burnt area on his back wasn't too bad, although it would need daily dressing changes with Silvadene cream applied.

When the emergency department doc finally released him, Lindsey realized he didn't have a way to get home.

"I'll give you a ride," she offered. "My shift is almost over anyway."

"Thanks." His voice was no longer hoarse, the oxygen with humidified air seemed to have done the trick.

She took Austin home and got him settled on the sofa. He preferred lying on his side to keep the pressure off the small burned area in the center of his back.

"Where's Josh?"

She gasped in horror. How could she have forgotten her son? Thankfully, it wasn't too late. "I'll get him from Tai Kwon Do." She hurried back outside to jump in her car, berating herself for the lapse. She really needed to pull herself together.

During the ride home she told him about Austin. "He was hurt during a fire, but he's home and will be fine."

"He was hurt?" Josh's eyes widened and alarm. "What happened. Did he get burned?"

"No, he's not burned," she hastened to assure him, skating over the truth. She should have remembered Josh had lost his father to a fire. And she should have taken more care in explaining Austin's injury. "He's fine, I promise."

The minute she pulled into the driveway, Josh rushed out of the car and ran into the house to see for himself.

She followed more slowly. She was grateful for Austin's influence on Josh, but it was clear her son had grown extremely attached to him.

She needed to move back into her own house as soon as possible, to protect her son from being hurt worse in the long run. Because she knew this being together with Austin was temporary.

No matter how much she secretly wished for more.

# CHAPTER NINE

Lindsey threw together a quick, early dinner, and then sat down to help Josh with his homework, fighting an insane need to check on Austin every three minutes.

Josh wasn't the only one who'd grown dependent on him. She'd grown accustomed to having Austin around as well. Despite her cheerful facade for Josh's benefit, she'd been worried about him too.

"Can I go and talk to Austin now?" Josh asked the minute he finished his math homework. His fourth-grade math homework that was almost over her head. What was she going to do when he reached high school? She dreaded thinking about it.

"Don't wake him up if he's sleeping," she cautioned. "He was up most of the night, working."

She wasn't surprised when Josh returned a few minutes later, his shoulders slumped with disappointment. "He is sleeping, Mom. Are you sure he's okay? He's gonna wake up right?"

"Yes, Josh, of course he's going to wake up." Aching for her son's obvious distress, she gave him a quick hug. "Please stop worrying. You know his shift requires him to work twenty-four hours straight. You would be tired too if you were up all night."

"I guess." Josh didn't look convinced. "Maybe I shouldn't go to Tony's house this weekend."

Now she knew Josh was seriously concerned. There wasn't anything that would have caused him to consider giving up going to his friend's birthday party. She understood his reservation, but she thought it would be best for Josh to go to Tony's. "Why don't you talk to Austin about it later?" She suggested, knowing he would encourage Josh to go and have fun. "Then you can decide what to do."

Her plan worked. Austin awoke a few hours later and she asked Josh to carry in his dinner tray, giving the two of them a chance to talk alone.

Sort of alone. She hovered in the hallway, listening.

"I was worried you weren't ever going to wake up," Josh said.

"Hey, I'm fine." Austin injected confidence in his tone. He sounded a hundred percent better from when she'd first seen him in the hospital emergency department. "Just tired from being at work for so long."

"That's what Mom said." There was a brief pause and then Josh added, "I don't know if I want to go to Tony's birthday party tomorrow."

"Why not? Did you and Tony have an argument?" Austin sounded surprised.

"No, I thought I should stay home because you're hurt."

"Josh, I promise I am not hurt. You should go to Tony's house for the party. He's expecting you to be there. You'll have lots of fun. And besides, I have your mom, the best nurse in the state to help watch over me."

"Are you sure?"

"I would be sad if you didn't go," Austin said firmly.

Satisfied, Lindsey hurried into the kitchen. Josh joined her a minute later. "He said I should go," Josh informed her. "He's really fine."

Refraining from stating the obvious—*I told you so*—she nodded and smiled. "Good. Get your things together so that we have everything ready to go by tomorrow." The plan was for Josh to go home with Tony Friday after school and stay overnight for the party on Saturday.

"Okay!" Josh ran to his room.

She had taken advantage of the chance to work a double shift on Friday, since Josh wouldn't be home. It had been a long time since she'd done sixteen hours straight, but the overtime would help cover that first large payment on her new loan. Austin would be okay in her absence; she would do his dressing change early in the morning before she left and then check it again later that night when she was home.

A win-win, she told herself. All she had to do was to ignore the small part of her that wanted to stay home to spend time with Austin.

---

LINDSEY HAD FORGOTTEN how busy Friday nights were in the emergency department. Since going back to work after Josh had started school, she mostly worked day shifts or the occasional weekend if Sam was going to be home.

But Friday nights were crazier than any other night of the week.

At least keeping busy made the long sixteen hours of her double shift go faster.

She started to wonder if it was a full moon when the

police brought in several behavioral health patients. Her admission was some guy who'd stripped down to his bare butt while standing in the middle of the street, talking to himself. When the police had arrived and asked him to put his pants back on, he'd begun to swear loudly, arguing with them and generally acting crazy. Assuming he needed medication of some sort, they brought him in to be evaluated.

Good thing they'd gotten him to put his pants back on first.

The police officer who brought in the behavioral health patient was Officer McDonald. Sean McDonald was a nice guy who she knew was a single parent, too.

"Hey, Lindsey, how are you?" He asked with a tired smile.

"Doing well, thanks. How about you? How's your daughter?"

"Much better." His daughter, Morgan, was older than Josh, in her early teens. Sean had talked about her on more than one occasion as she was obviously struggling with the loss of her mother.

"I'm glad." She tucked a strand of her long blonde hair that had come loose from her ponytail, behind her ear. "Is there a full moon out there or what? Could you please stop bringing in behavioral health patients?"

"Do you think we're having fun?" Sean joked. "Like I want to see some naked guy with his pants off?"

That made her laugh.

"Lindsey, are you doing anything next weekend? I'm off work and thought maybe we could go out for dinner or something."

What? She stared at him, completely taken aback by his invitation. No one had asked her out since Sam's death. She and Sean had always been friends, he'd never hinted at wanting more. She wasn't sure who was crazier, the guy who'd taken off his pants in the middle of the street or Sean McDonald. "Ah, thanks, but I don't think so."

"I understand," Sean said quickly, his face turning red. "I just thought, seeing as we're both single parents, that maybe... Never mind."

"It was sweet of you to ask," she said, not wanting him to feel bad. "I'm really sorry, Sean, but I'm just not ready."

"That's alright. Although if that being ready to date again changes, give me a call." He handed her a business card with the police department logo, his name and personal cell number on it.

Bemused, she took Sean's card, watching as he strode away. Sean McDonald was a nice looking guy but she wasn't remotely interested in going out with him. Or with anyone.

The thought of kissing any man that wasn't Austin, left a sour taste in her mouth.

She closed her eyes and rubbed her temple. How had this happened? How had she managed to get hung up on the one guy who was totally wrong for her?

Sean McDonald was a single parent, just like her. He'd been married before and knew what he was getting into. Just like her. Sean knew about marriage and relationships.

Austin was a guy who'd played the field, never settling down in a serious relationship. He had no idea what it was like to be a husband or a father.

So why couldn't she find a way to get him out of her system?

LINDSEY WAS EXHAUSTED by the time she returned to Austin's house just before midnight, but that didn't stop her from immediately heading down the hall to the master bedroom to check on him.

He was still awake, glancing up at her when she walked in. His chest and shoulders were bare, but he had the covers pulled up for modesty. "How was your shift?"

"Wicked." She was happy to see he appeared back to normal. "There's a full moon so you know what that means. Lots of behavioral health patients."

He grimaced in sympathy. "Bummer. I'm sure that wasn't easy."

"It's worth it for time and a half. Are you ready for your dressing change?" She glanced at the small stack of sterile dressings on his dresser.

"Sure." He didn't move right away, though, but continued to hold her gaze. "I really appreciate your help with this. If I could reach behind my back to do these dressing changes myself, I would."

"I know." She really did understand. "I don't mind." After the way he had rescued her from her neighbor's fire and brought her here to live with him, she was glad the shoe was on the other foot for once. It felt good to be the one helping him, rather than the other way around. "Turn over so I can reach your back."

He quirked a brow but did as she asked, flipping over onto his stomach and scrunching the pillow beneath his chest. The muscles rippled in his arms and she had to swallow hard and avert her gaze to focus on the reason she was here.

His wound. Dressing changes.

Wiping her hands on her scrub pants, she gingerly sat on the edge of his bed. "Peeling tape off," she warned as she gently stripped the old dressing off his back. She didn't have a vast experience with burns, but they oozed a lot and the thick dressing was soaked.

He didn't make a sound but she could tell his muscles were tense as he braced himself. He was fortunate the burn wasn't worse—the pink area looked relatively healthy, without any sign of infection.

"This looks really good," she told him.

He grunted. She stood and went to his adjoining bathroom to wash her hands and fetch a washcloth, soap and water. After cleaning the area, she patted it dry and then drew on gloves to apply the Silvadene cream.

Throughout the entire procedure, Austin didn't say a word. She wasn't sure if it was because the dressing changes hurt worse than he let on, or if he just couldn't think of anything to chat about.

She'd just finished taping the new dressing over the cream when he let out a low groan.

"What is it?" Then she saw his right shoulder was quivering and she put a hand on his heated skin. "Muscle spasm?"

"Yeah," he said in a low gravelly voice. "It'll go away soon."

She wasn't sure that was true, the way the muscles looked to be jumping out of his skin. She stripped off her gloves and quickly ducked into the bathroom to wash her hands then came back out to sit beside him. No way could she just sit there and watch as he writhed in pain.

All nurses were taught some simple massage techniques. She wasn't an expert by any means, but she figured anything was better than doing nothing. When she began to knead the sore muscles he groaned again, but this time she could tell it was a murmur of appreciation.

Massaging his neck and shoulders was awkward while sitting on the side of his bed. Her own back muscles began to scream in protest, so she got up and climbed on the bed, bracing her knees and either side of his waist. The position was a little embarrassing, but she decided to maintain a professional attitude.

She was helping to relieve his muscle spasm, nothing more.

Of course, she would have had to be dead not to notice his muscles. The breadth of his shoulders. The firm flesh of his biceps and the musky scent of his skin.

As he relaxed, her kneading strokes became longer, smoothing over his muscles with less pressure than she'd applied before.

"Lindsey," he croaked in a low voice. "You're killing me. Don't stop."

She had to laugh at the way he'd contradicted himself. His muscles were better, and she knew there was no reason to keep touching him.

Full of regret, she pulled her hands from his skin and climbed off him. He reached out to snag her hand. Then he rolled over to look up at her. "I'd like to kiss you."

"I—uh, we can't." She wanted to but knew that was only asking for trouble. Deep trouble.

Regret flashed in his eyes, but he instantly let her go. "Okay. I promised no strings and I meant it."

She admired his restraint. It was almost better than hers. She drew in a ragged breath. "Goodnight, Austin."

"Goodnight, Lindsey. Sweet dreams."

She slipped from his room, pausing to lean weakly against the wall. Austin had gotten under her defenses because she was physically and emotionally exhausted from her sixteen-hour shift.

She needed to stay strong. This—whatever she had with Austin wouldn't last. His relationships never did.

With an effort, she pushed herself to return to her room. Josh would be home tomorrow at four o'clock in the afternoon.

Surely, she could handle being with Austin alone for that long.

---

AUSTIN FELL asleep but awoke feeling guilty for how he'd once again taken advantage of the situation. Lindsey and Josh were his guests. He shouldn't have asked her for a kiss while she cared for him, especially after she'd worked a long double shift.

The biggest problem was that he didn't want to fight his feelings for her anymore. Was there a song about that? Maybe. It didn't matter. Just because he was falling in love with her, didn't mean she felt the same way.

He replayed her blunt and horrified refusal to his marriage proposal through his memory as he rolled out of bed. After washing up in the bathroom, he padded to the kitchen.

Lindsey was seated at the table, nursing a cup of coffee. She didn't meet his gaze, which only made him feel like a bigger jerk.

"I'll make breakfast," he offered brightly. He strode to the fridge and rummaged for what he'd need.

"I can help," she offered.

"Nope. I have it under control." He desperately longed for things to go back to normal. Whatever normal was between them.

Then he realized that wasn't what he wanted at all.

He swung toward her. "Lindsey, could we please talk?"

Before she could respond, a cell phone rang. Comically, they both searched for their respective phones. He assumed the call was for her because who else would be calling him bright and early on a Saturday morning? Maybe something was up with Josh.

But when he pulled out his cell phone, he saw his younger sister Amber's name on the screen. He quickly answered. "Amber? What's up?"

"Austin, I'm so glad you answered." Her normally cheerful voice was somber. "Dad suffered a heart attack last night. He's being prepped for open heart surgery."

# CHAPTER TEN

"What happened?" Austin gripped the phone so tightly he was surprised it didn't crack under the pressure. Details. He wanted details. His dad, Abe Monroe had always been so hale and hearty. It was his mother who'd suffered a broken hip two years ago and had gone through a long rehab and recovery to get back on her feet. Now she suffered from arthritis, too. His dad had prided himself on staying in shape. He saw his primary care doctor regularly, took his blood pressure meds as ordered and didn't overindulge in food or alcohol.

How was it possible his father was on his way to the operating room for cardiac bypass surgery?

"He had chest pain. At first, the cardiologist thought they could just place a stent to open his coronary artery," Amber said. "But they found three different blockages and decided it would be better if he went straight to the operating room."

He wasn't a doctor but even he knew that emergency surgery meant his father's condition was serious. His dad would need a triple bypass to stabilize his heart. Without hesitation he said, "I'll be there as soon as I can arrange a flight to Milwaukee."

"Good. We're at Trinity Medical Center," Amber informed him. "We'll be here in the family center until we hear from the doctor. I know you can't use your cell phone on the plane, but we'll call and leave a message once we receive an update on his condition."

"That works. I'll text you with my flight information, so you know when to expect me." He paused, then added, "Thanks for calling."

"Of course. See you soon."

He ended the call to find Lindsey watching him closely.

"Who's sick?" She asked, a sympathetic frown furrowing her brow.

"My dad." His own chest was starting to feel tight. Sympathy pains, maybe? Both of his sisters, Amber and Andrea were nurses. Most of his family was in the medical profession in some way. Except for his brother Alec, who was a cop, a sergeant with the Milwaukee Police Department. Alec had been smart enough to marry a doctor and, heaven knew, Jillian had plenty of physician connections at Trinity Medical Center.

His dad was in good hands.

Suddenly he missed his family very badly.

"Austin?" Lindsey came toward him and placed a reassuring hand on his arm. "What's wrong with your dad?"

He belatedly realized he'd never discussed his family with her. Not for any particular reason, he wasn't ashamed of them or anything. But the subject had not come up. Until now. He swallowed hard. "According to my sister Amber, he's had a heart attack. They were going to try and place a stent but he had three arteries blocked so they decided to take him straight to the OR for open heart surgery. I need to go home."

"To Milwaukee? You mentioned getting a flight there."

"Yeah." He pulled himself together and focused on her compassionate gaze. "Will you come with me?"

"Me?" Her voice squeaked in surprise.

"Yes, you. And Josh, too." He didn't want to analyze his feelings too closely, but knew he needed Lindsey there. At his side. He couldn't imagine facing this alone.

He couldn't even imagine his life if his dad didn't make it through surgery. He silently prayed for God to heal his dad and to guide the surgeon's hand for the best possible outcome for this procedure.

---

"WHY?" She asked before she could stop herself. She hadn't slept well haunted by the memories of kissing Austin. And wishing she had not denied his request for another kiss. Then she'd wondered if she was just like her mother. Allowing her out of control hormones to guide her decisions.

But her confused feelings were no longer important. Austin's father was undergoing emergency open heart surgery. He obviously needed a friend.

"Please? I need your support." His eyes darkened. "In case God calls my dad home."

"Your dad will be fine," she said with confidence she didn't feel. She didn't know anything about his father. But she was secretly thrilled that Austin wanted her near him in this time of crisis. "Of course, I'll come with you."

"And Josh?"

She hesitated, debating about whether she should bring

Josh. If she called Tony's mother, she was pretty sure Becky would agree to keep Josh while they were gone. On the other hand, she had no idea how long they'd need to stay in Milwaukee—much of that depended on how well Austin's father did after surgery. As the next week was a short week for school, the kids were off Thursday and Friday for teacher in service days, Josh wouldn't miss too much if she pulled him from class.

"We will both come with you," she decided. Josh would be upset if they kept him out of the loop. She knew her son would want to be there for Austin, too. "I'll call Tony's mother, to let her know we'll pick him up early."

"I'll make the plane reservations on the first available flight." His expression was dazed, as if the reality hadn't quite hit him yet. He turned and crossed to the living room where his computer was located to book the flight while she pulled out her phone.

After explaining everything to Becky, she then talked to Josh. He was great, didn't seem to be upset about missing the rest of Tony's party. Josh had sounded concerned about Austin and was more than willing to take this trip to Milwaukee.

She then had to call work to arrange to be off. Not an easy feat—especially after she had picked up the extra hours to begin with. She tried not to think about the large loan payment she would have to make as she called several of her colleagues to help cover her shift. Thankfully, one of the nurses she had done a favor for a few months ago came through and agreed to work in her place.

Five and a half hours later, they were at the gate, waiting to board their flight.

Josh's fascination with the process, his first time ever flying in a plane, was enough to keep them from worrying about what was going on in Milwaukee. But once they were seated on the plane, Austin reached over to take her hand in his.

She stared at their entwined fingers for a long moment. She had taken the middle seat between Austin and Josh, giving her son the window seat so he could enjoy the thrill of flying. Even though Josh was sitting right there, able to see how they were holding hands, she couldn't make herself let go. Clearly Austin was shaken by his father's abrupt illness. She would not deny him this small bit of support.

She tried to think of a safe topic to discuss. "You mentioned your sister, Amber. Do you have any other siblings?"

A faint smile tugged at the corner of his mouth. "Yeah. There's a few of us." He was quiet for a moment before glancing at her. "Are you sure you want to hear all this?"

She nodded. "Why not? We have plenty of time."

He nodded. "Amber is the baby of the family, two years younger than I am. She's married to a physical rehab physician by the name of Nick Tremayne. I'm next in line. Then there's Alec who is a cop. He's a year older than I am and married to Jillian. Jillian is an emergency medicine doctor at Trinity Medical Center. That's where my dad is, by the way. Then there's Adam, he's a couple years older than Alec and works as a pediatrician in his own practice. He recently got engaged to Krista Vaughan, one of the pediatric nurses at Children's Memorial Hospital."

"Wow," she murmured, when he paused for a breath. "How am I ever going to keep them straight?"

"Don't even try. My parents used all names starting with the letter A which only adds to the confusion. Where did I leave off?" He frowned. "Oh yeah, Adam. Andrea is the second oldest of the group. She's a nurse too and is married to a guy named Stuart who travels a lot as a pharmaceutical sales rep. They have two kids, Bethany and Ben. Oh, I forgot to mention, Alec has daughter too, Shannon who is a year younger than Bethany. They are both younger than Josh," he added glancing over to where the boy's face was plastered against the window. "Shannon is six and Bethany is seven to his nine but they're good kids. At least Josh will have someone to hang out with. Even if they're girls."

She chuckled. "That's good." The name of Austin's family were buzzing around in her head, making her dizzy. She mentally counted backward. "So there are five of you."

"No, six. The oldest is my brother Aaron. He's a big time orthopedic surgeon at Johns Hopkins institute. We don't see him very much. He was married, but he and Morgan divorced two years ago. They didn't have any children."

From what he described, Aaron's divorce was the oddity in a family who seemed to be all happily married. Except for Austin himself, that was. Hearing about his family now, she wondered why he had been satisfied with having a string of girlfriends, none of them serious. Had something happened in the past to make him a relationship shy? She wished she were bold enough to ask. "Your family sounds wonderful."

"Yeah. They are." His expression was solemn. "Our family is a testament to my parents. We were very blessed and had a great life growing up. My parents taught us about faith and God. They were wonderfully supportive and of course cared about us. Yet it was even more obvious the way they loved and doted on each other. My dad was pretty freaked out when my mom tripped over their dog Murphy, falling down the stairs and breaking her hip a few years ago." His eyes darkened. "I can't imagine what she's going through right now."

The way he spoke about his parents, and the love they had for each other, brought a lump to her throat. He was close to his family, much closer than she would have believed, considering the thousands of miles between Sun Valley, California, and Milwaukee, Wisconsin.

The lump in her throat swelled to the point she feared she might choke as realization sank deep. If something bad happened to his dad, would Austin want to stay?

Was it possible he would consider moving back home for good?

THEY ARRIVED IN MILWAUKEE LATE, almost eight o'clock at night, partially because of the two-hour time difference between California's Pacific Standard time and Wisconsin's Central Standard time. As Austin arranged for a rental car, she tried to explain the whole time zone thing to Josh.

"Back home it's still only six o'clock at night?" He asked, a puzzled frown in his brow. "I don't get it. How can it be one time here and another time someplace else?"

She launched into a discussion about time and the way it continually changed around the world. The more she talked the more she struggled to explain. Austin returned before she could confuse herself even more. She rested her hand on Josh's shoulder. "Just trust me, the time is different all around the world. In the US it's only a few hours from one side of the country to the other, but in Tokyo or Australia it's more than half a day."

Josh mulled this over as they threw their carry-on

luggage into the back of the rental car. "I still don't get it," he mumbled.

At this point, she wasn't sure she did, either.

Austin headed straight to the hospital where he quickly found his siblings in the family center, which turned out to be a common gathering place for people waiting to hear about loved ones coming out of surgery and those waiting to visit patients in the intensive care unit.

"Austin." A pretty woman that she thought was probably Amber ran over to give him a big hug. "Dad made it through surgery just fine. Did you get my message?"

"Yeah, I listened to it the moment we landed. Thanks for the call." He took Lindsey's arm and drew her forward even though she tried to hang back to give him space. "This is Lindsey Winters and her son Josh. Lindsey this is Amber and the rest of my family."

The Monroe group took up a large corner of the waiting room. She glanced over the sea of faces and easily picked out the Monroe brothers from the crowd because of their striking resemblance to Austin. "Hi."

"Welcome, Lindsey." An older woman approached, her gait stiff and her expression drawn but with a friendly smile on her face, nonetheless. "I'm Alice Monroe, Austin's mother. It's wonderful to meet you. I just wish it could be under different circumstances."

"I'm so sorry to hear about your husband," she murmured, feeling as if she didn't belong here with these people in their time of grief.

"Well God has carried him through surgery, so I am hopeful he will recover just fine." Alice sounded confident. The rest of the family nodded in agreement.

"Can I go up and see him?" Austin asked.

Amber nodded. "Sure. Andrea and Stuart are up there

now. We've been taking turns," she explained. "They don't want the entire family up there all at one time. I'll talk to the nurse and ask her to send Andrea and Stuart down so you can go up."

"Thanks, sis."

Josh was uncharacteristically shy, standing close to her side. She noted the two girls sitting next to each other and a young boy who looked to be about four or five playing a video game on the setup located in the corner of the waiting room. She turned to her son. "The two girls are Bethany and Shannon, and the little boy is Ben. Why don't you see if you could play Ben's video game with him?" She gave her son a gentle nudge. "I'm sure he won't mind."

"Will you come up to the ICU with me?" Austin asked in a low voice, when Amber got off the phone with the nurse. "I might need you to explain a few things."

She wasn't a critical care nurse, but she nodded anyway. "Of course."

Josh crossed over to join Ben, leaving her to follow Austin up to the third-floor cardiac intensive care unit.

He held her hand during the elevator ride up. His muscles tensed as they found the intensive care unit and walked through the main doorway. His dad was in the room right next to the nurse's station.

She heard Austin draw in a swift breath, and she didn't blame him for his horrified reaction. His father was connected to a ventilator and there were numerous IV pumps around his bed. His heart rate, blood pressure, and pulmonary artery pressures were all displayed on a monitor over his head. His dad's eyes were closed, and she felt Austin hesitate, as if he didn't want to go into the room.

A cute blonde nurse hurried over. "Hi, my name is

Tiffany and I'm Mr. Monroe's nurse for this evening." Her gaze zeroed in on Austin. "You're one of his sons?"

He nodded, his gaze never wavering from his dad's prone figure. "I'm Austin. How is he?"

"Doing really well. We're weaning him off the medications to keep his blood pressure stable, and we're also slowly weaning him off the ventilator." She turned to look at her patient. "I know there's a lot of equipment in the room, but he's doing fine. We refer to his condition as critical but stable."

He finally turned his gaze to the nurse. "Can he hear us?"

"He's been sleeping a fair amount, from the pain medicine and the anesthesia. But if you call his name, he'll open his eyes."

Lindsey urged Austin closer. "Come on come on take his hand and talk to him, so he knows you're here."

Austin hung back, resisting. "I don't want to bother him if he's sleeping."

"Most patients rarely remember much of the first night of their intensive care unit stay," Tiffany explained. "Go ahead. It won't bother him. I've noticed he's calmer when his family is around."

She'd said exactly the right thing to make Austin step closer to the bed. He gingerly took his dad's hand in his. "Hi, Dad. It's me, Austin. Can you hear me?"

His father opened his eyes and slowly turned his head to see his son. As their gazes connected, the older man nodded.

"I know you can't talk with that breathing tube in your throat, but I want you to know that I'm here and I love you." Austin's voice was low and thick, as he was trying hard to keep it together.

Her eyes pricked with tears as Abe Monroe nodded again trained to smile around the breathing tube in his mouth. His heart squeezed even tighter when the older man clutched his son's hand as if he would never let it go.

---

THE NEXT DAY, Lindsey found herself back in the family center, seated among the rest of the Monroe family. Aaron had surprised everyone by flying in from Boston which added a new level of chaos.

Everyone was so nice, putting her at ease and including her in their conversation. She was just starting to remember some of their names and linking them to faces, which, considering the size of Austin's family, was no easy feat.

She was seated beside Austin when his brother Adam, the pediatrician she remembered, strolled over.

"Hey, Austin. I see you finally got a girl of your own, huh?" Adam's eyes swept over her with a frankly admiring glance. "I like her. She's pretty."

She braced herself, waiting for Austin to correct his brother's erroneous assumption, but he didn't. "Thanks. I like her, too."

Unsure of what to say to that, she simply smiled weakly and held her tongue. Austin had asked her to come with him for support because, like a typical health care professional, he'd expected the worst. But his dad was making amazing process. They'd already gotten word that they'd taken out his breathing tube first thing that morning.

There was no point in reading more into Austin's motives for asking her to come along. And it was possible that he just didn't want to go into detail about their convoluted relationship. She couldn't really blame him. She wasn't really she wasn't sure how to describe it either.

Did they even have a relationship? She had no clue.

Austin could have any woman he wanted. And he proved that by dating half of the emergency department staff back in Sun Valley. He was an expert at short term relationships. She had to remember that there living under the same roof was a matter of convenience. Nothing more.

Yet being included in the Monroe gathering, as if she were actually a part of the family, gave her a strange sense of belonging. Growing up an only child, dragged from one of her mother's failed relationships to the other had made her feel isolated. Alone. She'd never experienced the warm, loving support or the overwhelming teasing of the Monroe family.

She secretly wished she and Josh really did belong here.

"How's Krista?" Austin asked.

Adam's entire face lit up. "She's amazing. She'll be here soon." Adam's expression turned serious. "I pray Dad will be able to make it to our wedding."

"He will," Austin assured him.

She remembered meeting Krista last night; she was Adam's fiancée. She wanted to ask when the wedding was taking place but didn't.

A few minutes passed before Alec called, "Austin? Can you come over here for a minute?"

"Sure." Austin flashed an apologetic glance, then stood and crossed over to where the brothers were having a quiet discussion. The moment his seat was vacant, Amber slipped into it.

"So, Lindsey, how long have you been seeing my brother?" She asked bluntly.

"Ah..." She glanced helplessly at Austin, but he was

already deep in conversation and not paying her any attention. "Not long."

"Oh." Amber's crestfallen face betrayed her disappointment. "We were all hoping you were different."

"Different?" She had no idea what Amber meant.

"Yeah, you know, different." Amber gave a philosophical shrug. "All of Austin's relationships are short lived. We were hoping the reason he brought you along all the way from California to meet us was that your relationship with him was something that might actually last."

# CHAPTER ELEVEN

Austin glanced over at Lindsey, catching a glimpse of the alarm in her gaze as Amber spoke with her.

Uh-oh. What was Amber saying about him? No doubt it was nothing good. He left Alec and Adam to discuss how they were going to support their mother while their dad was in the hospital and went back over to rescue Lindsey.

"Hey, are you ready to go up and visit my dad?" He quickly interrupted whatever Amber was saying.

"Sure." The way Lindsey jumped to her feet convinced him she was eager to leave. Sending his youngest sister a warning look, he took Lindsey's hand and walked out of the family center, down the hall toward the elevators.

"Did Amber say something to upset you?" He asked as they rode up to the third floor.

"No." She glanced away, not meeting his gaze.

Not good. "Please, don't pay any attention to my siblings. They get a kick out of teasing everyone. Sometimes their humor isn't as funny as they think it is. I promise they're harmless."

The elevator doors opened and they stepped off on the

third floor. Lindsey nodded but didn't say anything more as they entered the intensive care unit.

His mom was there, sitting in a chair next to his dad's bed. He flashed her a smile, then zeroed in on his dad, who still looked pale against the sheets. The breathing tube was out and there seemed to be less equipment in the room, two facts that eased his concern.

Maybe his dad was doing better after all.

"Hi, Mom." He approached the bed and took his father's hand. "Dad, how are you feeling?"

"Better, now that the breathing tube is out," he grumbled in a hoarse voice. "That tube was the worst part of the entire surgery."

His dad's chest had been cut open, his heart had been operated on, yet his biggest complaint was the breathing tube. Austin hid a grin. No doubt his dad hadn't liked the breathing tube because it had kept him from talking.

"As you can see, he's back to his feisty self," his mother added.

"Introduce me to your friend." His father's gaze landed on Lindsey.

"Dad, I'd like you to meet Lindsey Winters." He took her arm and drew her close to his father's bedside. "Lindsey this is my father, Abe Monroe."

"It's a pleasure to meet you," Lindsey said. "And I'm so glad you're feeling better."

"That makes two of us." His father grimaced. "Although they're not letting me go to a regular room until tomorrow."

"Tomorrow?" Austin frowned. "That's way too soon after such a major surgery."

"Not really," Lindsey countered calmly. "They usually try to get open heart surgery patients out of the ICU within

24 to 48 hours. Your dad will be one and a half days post-op once he leaves here."

"That's exactly what Cleo, his nurse said too," his mother confirmed with a serene nod.

"Hmm." Maybe so, but he still didn't like it. What if his dad took a turn for a worse on the regular floor? What if he suffered some sort of complication? The man's heart had been operated on, for Pete's sake."

"It'll be okay," Lindsey murmured, putting a reassuring hand on his arm as if she'd read his troubled thoughts. "They'll keep him on a continuous heart monitor on the post op cardiac surgery floor, enabling them to keep a close eye on his heart rhythm. The nurses are well trained for this sort of thing."

"I hope so." He was grateful Lindsey was there to help keep him grounded. Her knowledge as a nurse far exceeded his paramedic training, so he felt better knowing she wasn't as concerned about his dad going to the general floor.

He chatted with his parents for a few more minutes, but then sensed his dad was getting tired. "Dad, we're going to head back downstairs so you can get some rest." He glanced at his mother. "Mom, you've been up here all morning. Maybe you should take a break? It's almost time to for lunch."

His mother nodded. "I'll be down in a little while."

As they walked back to the elevators, Lindsey glanced at him. "I feel awkward, being here with your family. Maybe now that your dad is doing better, Josh and I should head home."

His footsteps faltered. "Please don't go yet. It's my family really that overwhelming?"

"A little." She smiled, but it seemed a bit forced. "Your family is fine. I'm not overwhelmed, I just don't want to intrude." After a moment's hesitation, she added, "But there's no rush for me to leave."

"Thanks." He gave her hand a quick squeeze. She belonged there with him and his family. "I really appreciate you sticking around to help me through this."

They hadn't had a chance to talk, but he vowed to have a serious discussion with her soon. She needed to know how much he cared. How much he'd fallen in love her.

Somehow, he needed to figure out a way to convince her to stick around, permanently.

---

LINDSEY FOLLOWED Austin back down to the family center, not sure if she was doing the right thing by staying with him in Milwaukee. All this togetherness was a bit much.

Yet it was difficult to convince herself to leave when he'd asked her so nicely to stay. Even though she felt like a fraud, pretending to be Austin's girlfriend, she really loved being treated as part of the family.

Josh and Ben were back playing video games. Her stomach growled, betraying her hunger. They hadn't had much for breakfast, just a quick bagel that seemed like hours ago.

After a few minutes of trying to ignore her stomach, others began to admit they were hungry too. She pried Josh away from the video games as they made plans for lunch.

The Monroe clan trooped down to the hospital cafeteria together, the guys arguing over who's going to pick up the tab. In the end, each of the brothers jammed several twenty dollar bills into Aaron's hand and he paid the tab, no doubt making up the difference out of his own pocket.

She found herself seated between Jillian and Amber, with Andrea and Krista directly across from her. Austin was at the other end of the table, next to the kids. She thought it was very clever the way the women maneuvered the kids to be near the men, shifting the parental responsibility just a bit.

In her opinion, it was good for the guys to share in the task of child rearing. Sam had been a good father to Josh, but he'd pretty much left most of the discipline and involvement in school to her.

When Austin got up from his seat to help cut up Ben's food, she found herself wondering what sort of father he'd be. If he took after his father, Abe Monroe, she suspected he'd be wonderful.

"You know Ben looks a lot like Austin," she mused, noting the stark family resemblance.

"In looks, yes, but hopefully not in temperament," Andrea said with a frown. "At least, I hope not. Austin got into a lot of trouble when he was young."

"He did?" For some reason that surprised her. Sure, Austin was known to have a reputation with the ladies, but she had always considered him to be very responsible.

"Absolutely." Amber flashed a wicked grin as she joined the conversation. "I could tell you about the time he held a party at our neighbor's house when they weren't home because he had a key so he could water the woman's plants. Or maybe you'd rather hear about the time he hitchhiked down to Chicago because he wanted to see a rock concert but my parents had grounded him. Or maybe—"

"Stop." Lindsey held up a hand, trying not to laugh. "Really? He did all of that?" She shot Alice, the matriarch of the family seated at the head of the table, an awed look. "Your mother must be a saint."

"She is," Amber agreed. "Although only the boys gave her grief. I'm the angel of the family."

"No, you're not," Andrea interrupted. "I am."

"The only thing I remember about Austin was that he had a different girlfriend every week during high school," Krista, Adam's fiancée, interjected with a dry tone. "All the girls mooned over him."

"Yeah, well, that hasn't changed," Andrea pointed out.

Lindsey was forced to agree. Just walking through the cafeteria, several women's gazes had followed him. She frowned, glancing at Austin's sisters. "Are you saying Austin has never had a serious relationship?"

"That is correct." Amber rolled her eyes. "Not for lack of trying, at least on the women's part. He'd always been a bit of a loner, going out with lots of women but not really getting close to any of them."

"I see." Lindsey's stomach clenched her appetite fading. So much for her theory that Austin had been seriously burned by a woman in the past.

"Do you?" Andrea raised a brow. "Because, honestly, Lindsey, you're the first woman he's introduced to the family. Like, ever."

Shocked by the news, she could only gape. "The first?"

"Yes," Amber agreed. "So even though you haven't been seeing him very long, we were hoping you were the one to bring him to his knees."

"Amber," Jillian said in a shocked tone. "That's not very nice. You really don't want Lindsey or anyone to break his heart, do you?"

"Hey, he's the one known around town as the heart-breaker, not me." Amber raised a hand in defense. "I just think it would be nice to meet the woman who finally brings my brother down."

"Well you don't have to worry, we're not that serious," Lindsey managed. "No one is getting a broken heart, here."

"Too bad," Amber murmured.

As Austin's family laughed and joked, Lindsey felt worse and worse. She knew everything they said was true, and not meant in a vengeful way at all. Yet hearing about Austin's reputation in detail certainly did not make her feel any better.

Amber had called him a heartbreaker. His reputation at Sun Valley Community Hospital was the same.

Why would a loner heartbreaker suddenly want to saddle himself with a wife and son?

Very simply, he wouldn't. Her heart ached and she realized just how much she'd been hoping maybe Austin had changed.

She needed to remember that Austin was nothing more than a friend. He could never be the husband or father she needed.

AUSTIN GREW restless with the inactivity. He didn't mind visiting with his family, but the constant togetherness was wearing him down. He wished he and Lindsey had more time alone to talk, but it seemed there were always interruptions.

Still, he was relieved his father was doing better. The following morning, they'd been forced to wait much longer than usual in the family center, until his father had been settled in a private room on a regular telemetry floor. Even then, they couldn't go visit right away as he'd gone for some sort of test. Aaron and Adam, the two physicians in the group had grilled the surgeon at length, then appeared satisfied with the discussion. It wasn't until much later in the evening that Austin and Lindsey were able to go up to see him.

He was thankful Lindsey hadn't mentioned returning home without him. He didn't quite understand why she was so anxious to leave unless Amber had said something to her. From what he could tell, she was getting along great with his family. He would have liked nothing more than to have introduced Lindsey as his fiancée. He'd blown his last proposal because he'd blurted it out without any warning in the most non-romantic way possible.

Now that he knew she'd been planning to divorce Sam, he was confident he could win her over. He needed to be patient and to show her with actions how much she meant to him.

Josh, too.

Adam continued to give him a hard time, payback for the way he'd flirted with Krista right under his nose a few months ago. Austin couldn't really blame him. He supposed he deserved it. Adam and Krista certainly looked happy together.

The same way he felt around Lindsey.

He glanced at her as they rode the elevators up to the third-floor cardiac unit, where his father's room was located. Her expression was serious, and he wondered what was going through her mind.

When the elevator doors opened, he held his arm in front of the electronic eye so she could pass through first. She thanked him with a smile, then fell into step beside him as he headed to his dad's room.

"Hi, Dad," he said as they walked in. Finding himself eye to eye with his father made him stop abruptly. "Hey, look at you—up and walking around."

His dad made a face. "The nurses forced me to."

"That's because walking and moving after surgery is good for your heart, Mr. Monroe," Lindsey said with a gentle smile. "You're doing a great job."

"I still have the strength of a mouse," he muttered, sitting down in a chair next to his bed with a small groan. "I can't wait for them to spring me out of here. I'd rather recover at home, in my own bed with your mother beside me."

"Speaking of Mom, she'll be back in an hour or so," Austin informed him. His mother had been at his father's bedside nonstop during his hospitalization. "She ran home to check in on the neighbors who are taking care of Murphy. We offered to go bring the dog back, but I think she needed a break."

His father's grumpy expression softened. "She deserves a break after the way I scared her with this stupid heart thing."

Had scared all of them, he thought. "Yeah, you really did that on purpose, didn't you?" Austin said in a dry tone. "Don't worry, she's fine. You will be back home, spoiling your grandchildren, before you know it."

"Speaking of grandchildren, I hear Lindsey has a son named Josh." The older man's gaze zeroed in on her. "Why haven't I met this young man?"

"I... uh..." Helplessly she looked at Austin. He gave a little shrug. He didn't know who'd mentioned it, but there weren't many secrets in the Monroe family. "No reason," Lindsey said with a forced smile. "Of course you can meet him. He's downstairs entertaining Ben."

"Next time bring him up with you," his father said. Then winced and put a hand over his heart. "Wow, I feel like I've run a marathon rather than just walking up and down the hall a couple of times."

The way his dad's face had grown pale concerned him. Lindsey must have been worried too, because she stepped forward and took her dad's wrist in her fingers. "Let me check your pulse."

He glanced up, but unlike the critical care unit, there was no cardiac monitor in the room. They must have a remote location where the monitors are watched. "Lindsey?" He tried to hide his worry.

"Your heart rate is a little irregular, Mr. Monroe," she said in a calm tone. "We better get you back to bed."

"I'm fine," his dad protested, but leaned forward and pushed up from the chair to do as she asked.

He swayed and nearly toppled over. Austin rushed forward to grab his dad's arm when it looked like he might not make it. Between them, he and Lindsey managed to get him back into bed.

"I'll call the nurse." Lindsey pushed the button on the call right beside him.

Austin nodded. His dad's skin was cool and clammy. Without a stethoscope, he could only imagine what his heart rate was doing.

"What's wrong," he asked in a low tone. "Premature ventricular contractions? Ventricular tachycardia? What?"

"Nothing that dramatic," she assured him. "If I had to guess I'd say he went into atrial fibrillation. Very common for patients after undergoing open heart surgery."

He nodded, having recently read about that. The nurse came into the room, wheeling a portable monitor with her. He suspected his dad's abnormal heart rhythm had been picked up on the remote telemetry monitoring.

His father lay back on his pillow, his eyes closed, has usually ruddy skin pale.

"Mr. Monroe?" The nurse, Irene, leaned close. "Are you all right?"

"I don't feel so good." He kept his eyes closed. "Dizzy."

Austin was thankful they'd gotten him back to bed when they had. He worried his dad might be taking a trip back to the intensive care unit. He watched as Irene connected Abe to the portable monitor and then proceeded to check his blood pressure. Within seconds she was paging the doctor.

"Let's try some Metoprolol," the doctor ordered when he came into the room a few minutes later. Austin recognized the guy as Dr. R. Gaines, his dad's cardiothoracic surgeon. The doctor looked at Irene. "Did he get his scheduled beta blocker dose this morning?"

"No, the night shift nurse said his blood pressure was too low," Irene explained. "I'll give it to him right away."

The way Dr. Gaines clenched his jaw told Austin his opinion of that, but the doctor didn't say anything more. Austin could understand the surgeon's frustration. The article he'd read in the waiting room had described the importance of beta blockers post cardiac surgery and the problems some nurses caused by being too cautious and giving the medication.

Beta blocker medications were supposed to be held if the patient's blood pressure or pulse was too low. That was under normal circumstances. The article suggested that in post operative cardiac surgery patients, the nurse should wait an hour and check the vitals again after the patient had been up moving around. Otherwise holding back the dose for a lengthy period of time could result in irregular heart rhythms.

Like atrial fibrillation.

"Get the defibrillator ready in case this doesn't work," Dr. Gaines said in an authoritative tone. "We may have to cardiovert."

Not good. "I better call my mother," Austin said, knowing she'd never forgive him if something happened, and she wasn't here.

"Hold off just a minute," Lindsey suggested, placing her hand on his arm. He wanted to haul her close, to hug her and to lean on her for strength and support. "Let's see if the medication works."

He reluctantly nodded.

Sweat beaded on his dad's brow. He looked awful, as if his body definitely didn't like the irregular heart rhythm. After Irene had given his dad the medication, she'd brought in large red crash cart, a defibrillator sitting on top.

He tensed when he saw the crash cart. He knew enough to know the drawers were full of emergency medications and other equipment like breathing tubes that could be inserted back into his dad's throat if he stopped breathing. It was concerning the nurse was preparing for a full blown cardiac arrest.

*Please Lord Jesus, keep my dad safe in Your care!*

He clung to Lindsey's hand as he stared at the heart monitor watching the irregular beats of his dad's heart, praying the medication would help.

It didn't.

"Cardiovert with 50 joules," Dr. Gaines ordered.

Lindsey tugged Austin out of the way.

"Charging." Irene placed patches on his dad's chest, before returning back to the defibrillator. "All clear?" She waited a moment for everyone to step back from the bed before hitting the button.

His dad's body gave a little jump when she delivered the shock.

For an agonizing moment his father's heart paused then return to its normal rhythm.

Austin breathed a sigh of relief, but his hands still shook.

That had been a close call. Clearly, his dad wasn't out of the woods yet.

# CHAPTER TWELVE

Austin was exhausted by the time they left the hospital. After his father's condition had stabilized, he'd called his mom who had hurried in to see what had happened. There had been a lot of discussion between the nurse and Dr. Gaines, but in the end, they decided not to move his dad back to the intensive care unit.

Austin wasn't sure if that was the best idea. In the ICU they would watch him more closely. He didn't feel right leaving his father's bedside, but the nurses made it clear it was time to go. Even his mother wasn't allowed to stay overnight.

"Is your dad going to be okay?" Josh asked, when they finally climbed into the rental car.

"Yes, he'll be fine," he assured the boy. Too bad, he didn't feel as confident as he sounded. He caught Lindsey's gaze and his heart squeezed when she smiled at him.

He couldn't imagine going through all of this without her. During the crisis at his dad's bedside, she had been there, supporting him. She had taken control of the situation, knowing exactly what to do and what to say.

It was times like this that he couldn't imagine his life without her.

He drove back toward The Cozy Inn motel which was only a few blocks from his parents' home. He shared a connecting room with Lindsey and Josh. Since they've already grabbed a meal earlier in the cafeteria, there was no reason to delay going back.

After he'd parked the car, Josh ran ahead to unlock the door using his mom's key. He and Lindsey followed more slowly.

They paused outside the motel room door. "Are you sure you're going to be okay?" She asked with concern. "You've been through a lot."

He forced a smile. "It's been a little stressful but I'm fine. Do you have time to change my dressing?" Their connecting rooms had enabled her to do his morning and evening dressing changes.

"Of course. Give me a minute." She entered the room she shared with Josh, leaving him to step into his own room.

A few minutes later, she poked her head through the connecting doorway. "Ready?"

"Yes, thanks." He drew his t-shirt over his head and stretched out on his stomach.

Since the back rub incident, Lindsey hadn't spent any more time than necessary in changing the dressing over his burn wound, her touched professional and impersonal as if he were just another patient. This time was no different. Once she finished, she rose and took several steps back. "You're all set. The area looks like it's healing well."

"Good. Thank you." He rolled off the bed and reached for his shirt. He caught her staring at his chest for a moment, but then she looked away. He quickly drew his shirt back. "Thanks for being there today."

"That's why I'm here." Her tone was light, but she reached out to give his arm a light squeeze. "Goodnight, Austin. We'll see you in the morning."

"Goodnight, Lindsey." He fought the urge to crush her close, kissing her the way he longed to. But with Josh in the other room, that wasn't an option. He followed her to the connecting doorway but didn't close his side all the way. He told himself he wanted to be available if she needed anything.

For a moment he leaned his forehead on the door frame, wishing things were different. They'd been in Milwaukee for two days, but still hadn't had a chance to talk privately. As much as he loved his family, there wasn't a moment of alone time, between his siblings, their spouses and children, not to mention Josh.

Maybe he could persuade Alec or Andrea to watch Josh tomorrow night so that he and Lindsey could go out for dinner. A nice romantic meal. He was chagrined to realize they'd never really had a date. Not the two of them alone, without Josh.

Shaking his head at his idiocy he dropped onto on the edge of the bed. No wonder she hadn't taken his proposal seriously. He'd never even taken her out on a proper date. Obviously, he was losing his touch when it came to women. In truth, he'd never had to try hard to get dates. Often women approached him first, making it easy.

This was different. Lindsey had avoided him from the beginning. Keeping her dire financial situation a deep secret. She hadn't seemed to want anything from him, but that was slowly changing. Or so he hoped.

He couldn't bear to fail now.

Not when Lindsey mattered so much.

LINDSEY HAD trouble falling asleep but must have dozed a little because a noise woke her up in the small alarm clock on the bedside stand read quarter past midnight.

She took note of Josh's even breathing from the bed next to hers. She stared into the darkness wondering what had woken her up.

Then she heard it again a muffled thump from the room next door. Austin? She slid out of bed, shivering in her thin pajamas which were not made for the chilly Wisconsin spring weather, and making her way to the door connecting their rooms.

Feeling foolish she hovered near the opening, straining to listen. She heard a voice but it sounded deep, like Austin's, not the muted sounds of the television.

Was he talking to someone in his family? Had his father's condition changed for the worst? She wouldn't be at all surprised to discover the nursing staff at Trinity Medical Center had moved his father to the intensive care unit.

Biting her lip uncertainly, she debated going inside. Glancing over her shoulder, she made sure Josh was still sleeping, before reaching up to flip the lock on her side of the connecting door. She opened it, expecting his door to be closed and locked too.

It wasn't. She pushed the door further and stepped into Austin's room.

He stood next to the bed, wearing a pair of flannel pants and a T-shirt as he spoke with someone she presumed to be from the hospital. She must have made a noise because he swiveled around to look at her in surprise.

"Thanks, let me know if anything changes. Goodnight."

He ended the call and set his phone aside. "Lindsey? What's wrong? Trouble sleeping?"

"You're the one who's not sleeping." She crossed her arms over her chest, feeling self-conscious as she kept her voice low so as not to wake Josh. "I heard you bumping into things. What happened? Your dad?"

"He's fine. He managed a lopsided smile. "I'm sorry I woke you. I just wanted to check in on him. The night shift nurse assured me his vitals are stable and that he's been getting some badly needed sleep."

"That's great to hear." She wished there was more she could do, he wore his worry like a heavy winter coat. She knew better than most there were potential complications after surgery, especially something as major as undergoing a cardiac bypass procedure. "Maybe you should take something to help you sleep. You won't do your dad any good wearing yourself down."

Austin shook his head. "No, thanks. But I could use a hug."

The flash of vulnerability in his gaze caught her off guard. How could she refuse a simple hug? Two steps found her in his arms, her face buried in the crook of his neck, his face nuzzling her hair.

"I was so worried about him, but you were calm, cool, and collected when you checked his pulse," Austin murmured in her ear. "I'm glad you called the nurse when you did. Have I thanked you yet for coming along with me?"

Her heart swelled as she smiled against him. "Yes, you did. And I'm glad to be here." She held him close, reveling in his embrace, but then loosened her grip to step back.

Only he didn't let her go. Caught within the circle of his arms, she glanced up to find him staring down at her intently. Awareness sizzled between them. It was always like this with him. And she really didn't understand why. Before she could break away, he lowered his head and kissed her.

As before his kiss melted her resistance. He kissed her with the hunger mixed with desperation, as if he were afraid she would run if he let her go.

The problem was that she didn't feel at all like running.

His mouth was sweet, gentle but probing as he took his time kissing her. In some corner of her mind she knew she needed to get a grip before this desire simmering between them spiraled out of control.

But she didn't want to let Austin go.

He finally broke off their kiss but continued to cradle her close. "Lindsey, I'm falling in love with you."

Love? She leaned back to look up at him, not sure she'd heard him correctly. "You are?"

"Yes." His gaze searched hers with a breath stealing intensity. She desperately wanted to believe him. That this was the start of a real relationship. Not a rebound romance, the kind her mother had excelled at, but a real, based-on-love, relationship.

She wanted to respond in kind, telling him that she loved him, too. Probably more than she'd loved Sam. She and Sam had been too young to get married and becoming pregnant with Josh almost right away had added an additional strain to their new and fragile union.

Austin was different from Sam, in so many ways.

Yet a smidgen of doubt remained. Austin had played the field for so long, she found it hard to believe he really meant what he'd said. New line how is it possible that he'd suddenly fallen in love with her? And if so, why? How in the world was she any different from all the other women he'd ever gone out with?

"Lindsey, I asked you before and I haven't changed my mind so I'm asking you again. Will you please marry me?"

She sucked in a quick breath, her heart thundering in her chest. He may have asked her once out of misguided sense of wanting to help her, but twice? She didn't know what to think. "Why?" She blurted. "Out of all the women you've dated in the past, you never had a serious relationship. So why now? Why do you want to marry *me*?"

His expression turned grim. "My sisters did say something to upset you. I'm sorry, Lindsey. I can't lie. Amber and Andrea are right, I never dated anyone seriously before. But that was only because I never found anyone I wanted to spend the rest of my life with."

That was exactly what she was afraid of. "Sam always claimed you never dated the same woman more than once. I think he was jealous because he was stuck with me."

Austin's gaze darkened. "He was blessed to have you and Josh. Is that why you won't marry me? Because of Sam?"

"Not exactly." Her broken marriage was part of the issue. She couldn't bear the thought of going from one bad relationship to another. "My marriage with Sam was about to end. I told you I filed for divorce the day before he left to go on that last smoke jumping mission. And I know deep in my heart that my telling him what I'd done is the main reason he died that day."

"No, Lindsey that's not true. I should have told you this before." He hesitated, as if searching for the right words. "Sam's death wasn't your fault. It was mine."

"Yours?" She shook her head. "I don't believe you."

"Yes. My fault." He dragged his hands through his air, his expression pained. "I'm sorry. I should have come clean about what happened a long time ago."

"What do you mean? What happened?" She didn't understand what he was talking about. Smoke jumping was dangerous, and that much she knew. But Austin wasn't the reckless sort, not in the way Sam sometimes was.

Truthfully, she would have trusted Austin with her life.

"That day we were fighting the wildfire under dicey conditions. We were warned going in that the wind might shift, but they had predicted we had a solid twelve hours before that happened."

She nodded, silently urging him to continue.

"We were making headway against the fire. Sam was working north of me when suddenly the wind shifted coming up from the south. He was farther away in the clear, but I wasn't. The fire headed straight toward me. I figured my time was up, I had made my peace with God and was ready to be called home to be with Jesus. But then Sam appeared out of nowhere, telling me to run for the river. Even after we reached the water, Sam didn't quit. He kept on working, lighting a backfire to divert the path of the wild-fire. When he finally finished, we both jumped into the water. I was face down, but I don't think Sam was, or he didn't stay that way as long as he should have. The fire didn't get us, but he must have taken in a lot more smoke than I did because suddenly his breathing was bad. Very bad."

She couldn't speak, the picture he painted was far too real. Good heavens, she'd never realized how close Austin had come to dying that day, too.

"He'd inhaled too much smoke, but there was nowhere for us to go. I called the medevac chopper, and they did come for us, but it was too late." Austin's gaze was tortured. "Sam could have saved himself, Lindsey, but he didn't. He came back for me. And he died for his efforts."

She didn't know what to say. After all these months, she had honestly believed Sam had been careless. Had purposefully put his life on the line because she'd filed for divorce and had asked him to leave.

She'd built him up in her mind as being the bad guy. Especially after she discovered the mountain of debt he'd left behind. And she'd been angry at the way he'd tossed his life away, as if she and Josh hadn't been worth the effort.

Now Austin had just told her that in those final moments of his life Sam hadn't been careless after all.

He'd been a hero.

# CHAPTER THIRTEEN

Lindsey stared at him for a long moment, unsure of what to say. Truthfully, she was glad to hear that in the end Sam had come through when it had counted. That her husband had cared enough about Austin to help save his life.

"Can you forgive me, Lindsey?" Austin's tone held a note of anxiety. "I know I should have told you sooner, but I didn't want you to hate me."

"Of course, I don't hate you. And there's nothing to forgive. You and Sam were doing your best in a difficult and dangerous situation." She pressed her lips together in a self-depreciating frown. "How strange we've both been feeling guilty over the same thing. Each blaming ourselves for Sam's death."

"His last thoughts were of you," Austin said slowly. "He was worried about both you and Josh."

What was left of her anger evaporated. Sam may not have been the best husband, but he had cared. She nodded. "Thank you for telling me."

The expectant look he gave her made her realize she'd never answered his question about marrying him. And as much as she really wanted to, she just couldn't. Not yet. Everything was too confusing.

"I don't know if I can marry you, Austin," she finally admitted. "My heart wants to say yes, but my head is telling me I need time."

His smile was crooked. "I think you should listen to your heart."

She let out a chuckle. "I'll think about it, okay? I promise I'll consider your proposal."

Expecting an argument, she was somewhat surprised when he nodded. "That's all I'm asking, Lindsey. You can take all the time you need."

"Thank you." She turned and made her way toward the connecting door.

Austin moved quickly, catching her hand to stop her. "Lindsey?"

"Yes?"

He pulled her back into his arms for a thorough kiss. Her head was spinning by the time he let her go. "Think about that while you're considering my proposal," he murmured. "I'll see you in the morning."

"Okay." It wasn't easy to shake off the effect of his kiss, but she forced herself to go before she made another rash decision. She slipped through the connecting door to her room she shared with Josh.

He was still sleeping, thankfully. She eased into her own bed and stared up at the ceiling, mulling over Austin's marriage proposal.

Somehow it was difficult to remember the reasons she'd resisted saying yes.

THE NEXT MORNING, Josh was up early. Of course, he'd gotten a full night's sleep, unlike her.

Stifling a wide yawn, she padded to the tiny coffee maker filled it with water and stared as the carafe slowly filled with freshly brewed coffee.

The stupid machine dripped slower than molasses.

She'd finished two cups before she felt ready to face the day, hence they were later than usual for their normal breakfast routine.

Josh had gone through the connecting door to find Austin. After taking a shower and changing into fresh clothes, she pasted a smile on her face as she joined them. "Good morning. Are we ready to head out for breakfast?"

"Yeah!" Josh was practically bouncing on the bed he had so much energy. "Guess what, Mom? Austin says I'm going over to Mrs. Parker's house tonight for dinner."

"Mrs. Parker?" She frowned sliding an arched glance at Austin.

"My sister Andrea is having all the kids over for a pizza dinner," he quickly explained. "I figured you wouldn't mind if Josh joined them."

She didn't, except that he could have asked her first.

"This way you and Austin can go out for a fancy schmancy dinner." Her son comically rolled his eyes, making a goofy face before flopping back on the bed. "No kids allowed."

"Thanks for letting the cat out of the bag," Austin muttered.

"Cat?" Josh sat up and frowned. "What cat?"

"Never mind." She realized Austin had created this kid dinner just so they could go out. She couldn't help being impressed by his ingenuity. "Let's eat, shall we?"

Josh talked non-stop through breakfast, which was a

good thing because after the deep conversation with Austin last night, she was finding it difficult to get back on normal terms. Maybe it was just her imagination, but she was sure Austin kept sending her heated glances as if wanting to pick up their earth-shattering kiss where he'd left off.

No more kissing, she silently told herself as she concentrated on her food. She couldn't think straight when he kissed her like that.

When they had finished at the restaurant, Austin drove straight to the hospital. The plan was to visit for a while, then head back to his parents' house to get things ready for Abe Monroe's return home.

Aaron had booked an early flight back to Boston as he had surgeries scheduled. The rest chatted in the waiting room with the other family members as there were too many of them to descend on Abe at one time. Lindsey leaned over to Austin. "You might want to arrange for sub sandwiches or something for lunch," she whispered. "Otherwise, your mother is going to feel as if she needs to feed us, and she doesn't need that added stress right now."

"Good point." He turned to Amber and the two of them put their heads together over their phones to arrange for a box of sub sandwiches to be delivered to the Monroe home around noon.

Despite his arrhythmia episode the previous evening, she was thrilled Abe looked much better when they made their way up to visit. This time she brought Josh along so he could meet Austin's father. She rested her hands on her son's shoulders and smiled at the older man. "Mr. Monroe, this is my son Josh. Josh this is Mr. Monroe, Austin's father."

"You can call me Grandpa Monroe if you like," Abe offered. He was sitting in a chair dressed in a hospital gown and robe. "That's what the other grandkids call me."

Josh glanced up at her, silently asking permission and she gave a subtle nod. It was probably easier than using Mr. Monroe with so many other Mr. Monroes around.

"So what grade are you in at school?" Abe asked.

Josh went into a full discussion of what was currently happening in the fourth grade, and of course mentioned the Tai Kwon Do classes he and Tony were taking. Which led to a demonstration of his yellow belt "form".

As Josh displayed the series of choreographed moves, Lindsey had to admit she was impressed. Maybe Austin was right about the martial arts being all about self-control. And boosting self-confidence.

"You're not upset about dinner tonight, are you?" Austin asked, after they'd returned to the family center.

"No, although I was taken aback at first," she answered honestly. "It was sweet of you to make the arrangements."

Austin's grin faded. "I'm sorry it took me so long to realize we'd never really been out on a date by ourselves."

She shrugged. "Dating isn't easy as a single mom."

He nodded, but she could tell he was still troubled by the lapse. They made their way over to his parents' house where much of the family had already congregated.

Lindsey helped Amber and Andrea in making casseroles that would be placed in the freezer to make things easier for Alice after Abe returned home. The guys worked on setting up a room for their father on the first floor so he wouldn't have to navigate the steep staircase leading to the master bedroom on the second floor. The kids were relegated to play in the family room, basically with instructions to stay out of the way.

"Rats, the kitchen sink is blocked again," Amber said in exasperation. "This is the second time in two weeks. Lindsey, will you go ask Austin to come look at it?"

"Sure." Feeling as if there were too many cooks in the kitchen anyway, she was glad to escape. Austin's family was nice, but they made a simple project into a major production.

She found Amber's husband, Nick and Alec in the now and newly created downstairs bedroom putting the bed frame together. "Where's Austin?" She asked.

"Upstairs with Adam, they're working on the dresser." Alec flashed a grin. "Take a right at this top of the stairs."

"Thanks." She followed his simple directions, but her steps slowed as she neared the top of the stairs.

"Give me a break, Adam. I know what I'm doing. I can handle a little responsibility. I promised Sam I would take care of Lindsey and Josh."

She sucked in a harsh breath. Responsibility? Was that really how he viewed her and Josh—as a responsibility?

Because he'd promised Sam he would take care of them?

Dazed and nauseous, she turned away and stumbled into the nearest room, which happened to be the bathroom. She sank onto the commode before her knees gave out.

Why hadn't she put the pieces together before?

Austin had never been in a serious relationship. For years he'd hopped from one woman to the next, leaving a string of broken hearts in his wake. He could have any woman he wanted.

Why would a serious heartbreaker suddenly decide to settle down with a wife and son?

Only because he'd made a deathbed promise to his best friend.

It made so much sense now that she knew everything.

And the stark truth made her want to cry.

LINDSEY COULD BARELY PASTE a smile on her face for Austin's family, but the chaos over lunch helped her hide her feelings.

But she knew she couldn't stay. Especially not when Austin had planned a special dinner for them. When he headed out to get a new elbow pipe for the kitchen sink, she took her chance and ran.

Not literally, but she did call a rideshare.

"Will you tell Austin I had to go back to the hotel for a while," she said to Amber when she asked where they were going. "I'm not feeling well."

"Is there anything I can do to help?" Amber asked with a worried frown. "I'm sure Andrea wouldn't mind keeping an eye on Josh if you want to catch a nap.

"No, I'll be fine." The last thing she wanted was to leave Josh with Andrea. Not when she had every intention of packing up their belongings and heading out to the airport to catch the first flight to Los Angeles. Thankfully, Austin had purchased tickets for them to fly standby, since they hadn't known how long they'd be staying, so she didn't need anything from him.

Least of all a marriage proposal born of responsibility and a promise to her dead husband.

"Why are we leaving without Austin?" Josh asked, becoming obstinate when she told him to pack his bag.

"Because I need to get back home for work." It was easier to stretch the truth than to explain the personal issues between them.

"You had a fight, didn't you?" Josh demanded in a petulant tone. "I'm not going back. You can't make me."

Her temper flared. "Yes, you are! You are my son and I am telling you we are leaving. *Now*."

The shocked expression on his face when she yelled at him haunted her on their sullen ride to the airport.

Her mother had always taken her frustrations about her failed relationships out on Lindsey, too.

She felt sick, knowing she was following in her mother's footsteps in more ways than one.

---

AUSTIN SWALLOWED HIS FRUSTRATION. After fighting to clear the clog, he tried to get the pipe apart, only to crack the stupid thing. That had required a trip to the closest hardware store. After what seemed like forever, he finally had it replaced and working properly,.

With a sigh of relief, he crawled out from under the sink. One project finished. Maybe his brothers had moved all the furniture down from his dad's room in the hours he'd played plumber.

He cleaned up the mess and looked around for Lindsey. It was later than he'd thought, almost four in the afternoon. She wasn't in the family room with the kids. And neither was Josh.

After wandering through the various rooms in his parents' house, he discovered she seemed to have disappeared.

"Amber." He cornered his sister in the bedroom. "Have you seen Lindsey and Josh?"

"Oh, yes, I was supposed to tell you she went back to the hotel shortly after lunch. She said she wasn't feeling well."

What? Since when? "How did she get there?" He'd used the rental car to run to the hardware store.

"I think she called a rideshare." Amber frowned. "Although now that you mention it, I don't know why she didn't just ask one of us for a ride. We would have taken her back." His sister's gaze sought his. "Is everything all right?"

He had a bad feeling things were not all right. "I don't know. I'll head back to the motel to check on her."

Amber's worried expression cleared. "Good idea. Maybe the full extent of the Monroe family got too much for her. You mentioned she doesn't have any family of her own. We are a bit much to digest all at one time."

"Yeah. Maybe." He doubted that was the problem. Lindsey hadn't mentioned feeling overwhelmed by his family. Instead, he'd gotten the opposite impression. She seemed to enjoy having his sisters to talk to.

He made it back to the motel in record time. He went to Lindsey's room and rapped sharply on the door.

A man opened it. "Yeah? What do you want?"

Embarrassed, he stepped back. "Sorry, wrong room."

He spun around and marched back to the front desk. Only to be told no, Lindsey Winters had not requested to be moved to a different room. She'd checked out several hours ago.

He couldn't believe it. She'd left. She'd just up and left without him. Without saying a word. Had he pushed too hard? She said she'd consider his proposal. What on earth had gone wrong?

In a daze he returned to his room. There was an envelope with his name scrawled across the front, propped against the TV.

He snatched it up and quickly read her note. *Josh and I are not your responsibility, Austin. I know you promised*

*Sam you'd take care of us, but please believe me, Josh and I will be fine on our own. Thank your family for me. Take care of yourself, Lindsey.*

Responsibility? Promise to Sam? How in the world had she learned about his deathbed promise to Sam?

Then he knew. He'd mentioned it to Adam. She must have overheard him. His older brother had been giving him a hard time as usual. Adam had said something about how he'd better not drop Lindsey the way he had his other girlfriends, because she deserved better. Annoyed at his brother's assumption, he'd told Adam he'd loved Lindsey for years and knew what marriage was all about. Had assured him he could handle responsibility. He had only mentioned the promise he'd made because Adam hadn't taken him seriously.

He had not meant for Lindsey to find out the way she had. It was true, he had promised Sam he'd take care of her and Josh. But that wasn't why he wanted to marry her. He could take care of her without taking that step. He wanted to marry her because he loved her.

He stared at the note. She didn't believe in his love, that much was clear. But what he didn't understand was why. He told her he loved her and wanted to marry her. Even if she had overheard his comments about his promise and being responsible, why had a snippet of conversation overridden what he'd told her?

What else could he say to convince her?

Or was the real problem that she didn't love him back?

He tossed his clothes into his suitcase. He wanted to go straight back to Sun Valley, but first he needed to explain to Andrea that Josh wouldn't be coming for the pizza party and then he needed to see his dad one last time, just to make sure he was all right.

But once he did return home, he and Lindsey were going to have a long talk. There had to be a way to convince her of his love. He desperately wanted her to give their relationship a chance.

Because he could not imagine spending the rest of his life without her.

---

AUSTIN WAS jet lagged when he finally trudged to his car which he'd left at the airport. Flying standby by was a pain in the butt. He'd had to wait hours before he'd been able to find an available seat on a flight home. He hadn't seen Lindsey or Josh at the Milwaukee airport, so he could only assume they'd had better luck in finding a flight to Los Angeles than he had.

As he drove home, he thought about what to say to Lindsey. How on earth he could get her to believe him? Not only had he told her he loved her, but he's done his best to show that with his actions too. He'd kissed her. He'd brought her home to meet his family. He'd arranged for them to have dinner.

No woman had ever touched his heart the way she did. The more he thought about it during the long flight home, the more he had trouble believing she didn't feel anything for him in return. Something was holding her back. He wished he knew what that was.

His cell phone rang and he quickly glanced at the screen, hoping the caller was Lindsey. But, no, it was just Amber. His family had figured out something was going on when he told them Lindsey and Josh had left to fly home without him.

He let the call go to voicemail. As much as he loved his family, he couldn't talk to them yet.

What could he say when he hadn't even spoken to Lindsey?

When he pulled into his driveway, the house was completely dark. For the second time that day his stomach clenched. It was only eight o'clock at night. Were they already in bed, sleeping?

He threw the gearshift into park and jumped out. Without taking the time to grab his luggage, he unlocked the front door with his key. Flipping on the light switch, he looked around.

No note. Was that good or bad? He didn't know. As he walked through the kitchen, into the living room and then down the hall toward the bedrooms, there was no sign of Lindsey or Josh having been there.

When he opened the door to Lindsey's room, the bed was neatly made. When he walked over to the dresser and opened the drawers, they were completely empty.

The same for Josh's room. Lindsey and Josh had packed up their things and moved out.

Her message couldn't have been any clearer. As far as Lindsey was concerned, their relationship was over.

# CHAPTER FOURTEEN

The following morning, Lindsey drove a sulky Josh to school. He was mad that they'd come home on Tuesday, which meant not missing as much school. But the reality was that Josh was more upset because they'd left Milwaukee without Austin and with her decision to move them back home, despite the construction in progress.

"I'll pick you up at Tony's at four-thirty," she said when he jumped out of the car. She'd hoped the ability to go home with his friend for a while would smoothing things over.

"Whatever." To his credit he didn't slam the door, but she could tell he was clearly not his usual happy self, either.

Back home, she glanced around her bungalow with a feeling of satisfaction. When she'd woken up earlier today, she'd suffered a momentary pang of regret at how she'd moved out of Austin's house last night. But now she was convinced it was for the best. When she'd gone through the mail from while she'd been away, she discovered all the nurses at Sun Valley Hospital were getting a modest raise. Encouraged by the news, she did some household budget calculations based on her new salary.

If she was careful, she could pay the high interest loan payment by working just one extra shift in a two week pay period rather than two. Things weren't as bleak as she'd originally thought. And really, after everything that had happened with Sam, it felt good to have a home of her own, one she could afford and be responsible for.

She didn't need Austin's money. Didn't want or need him to feel responsible for her financial situation.

After cleaning up the kitchen area, she threw together a quick sandwich for lunch, trying to ignore the fine layer of drywall dust covering every other surface in the small house. On the positive side, she discovered the electrical work to bring the wiring up to code had been completed while they were gone, so the house was safe to live in from that standpoint. There were still quite a few drywall repairs to be made, but there was no reason she and Josh couldn't stay there while the work was being done.

No one had ever died from eating drywall dust, had they? She gave her sandwich a dubious glance but then took a big bite.

Maybe living in a construction zone would be uncomfortable but it certainly wasn't impossible. She would just have to do a little bit of extra cleaning every day, that's all.

And if it was lonely without Austin being around, she'd get over it. And so would Josh.

She sighed and put down her half-eaten sandwich. The impact of her rift with Austin on Josh was the toughest to take. No matter how hard she tried to tell herself they would have had to move home sooner or later, it wasn't easy. Josh was too important. He'd come so far, she would hate to see him regress. Regardless of what had transpired between her and Austin, she decided to ask him if he would keep in touch with Josh so her son didn't lose the connection to a positive male role model.

Josh deserved at least that much stability. And she didn't think Austin would refuse, as staying in contact with Josh would fulfill his promise to Sam. Win-win, right? She swallowed hard, reminding herself she didn't need anything from Austin.

The front door to her house abruptly swung open. When Austin strode inside, she jumped, knocking her glass of milk and spilling the contents onto her half eaten sandwich.

She grabbed the towel and quickly mopped up the mess. Stealing herself for an argument she opened her mouth to try and explain, but he swept her into his arms and kissed her senseless.

His mouth wasn't rough or angry but was deeply sensual. So much so it didn't take long for her to melt against him. Her head was spinning when he finally broke free.

"Are you really willing to throw this away?" He demanded in a husky voice.

She took a few steps back, grabbing onto the counter for support while trying to gather her scattered thoughts. She needed to make him understand.

"Austin, the first man I married was based on feelings I thought were love but probably weren't. Sam seemed like everything I wanted." She sighed. "But things quickly changed, and I learned that a marriage needed more than just affection. I refuse to make the same mistake again."

"You really think marrying me would be a mistake?" He looked hurt.

"Austin, please try to understand. When my marriage to Sam fell apart, I knew it was because we didn't love each other enough." She thought about how Austin's parents had interacted during the time of crisis, the way his whole family had pulled together. She wished she'd had that with Sam, or even with her own family. But she didn't. She hadn't even seen her mother since she'd left home and enrolled at nursing school. The last she had heard, her mother had moved to Colorado with her latest boyfriend. To say she and her mother were not close was a gross understatement. "Sam and I did not have what your parents do."

Austin was silent for a moment. "Maybe you did marry Sam when you were young, but Sam always seemed to be happy. He never mentioned anything about being dissatisfied with your marriage."

That surprised her. With the way Sam had chafed against the responsibilities of marriage especially toward the end, she would have thought he'd have confided in his best friend. "I guess I'm glad he didn't say anything to you, but the end result was the same."

"What result? What happened, Lindsey. Why did your marriage fall apart?" His earnest expression convinced her he really wanted to know.

She shook her head, wondering how to respond. "There wasn't any specific incident, we just stopped loving each other." How could she make him understand something she didn't quite know herself? "Don't you see? That's what concerns me. There wasn't any one major thing. We drifted apart, but I didn't even know about his gambling problem until after he died." She drew a shaky hand through her hair. "Sam wasn't a horrible person, he didn't hit me or hurt me. But I didn't love him enough. I think maybe he sensed that. And in the end, I wanted something more from my life than an empty marriage."

"You deserve more out of your life than an empty

marriage," he agreed, a puzzled frown in his brow. "I wish I'd known about his debts, though. That was something else he kept from me."

"That makes two of us." She sighed. "It's embarrassing to admit, but I always let Sam take care of the bills. And look where that got me? I guess it's one of the reasons I'm so determined to remain independent."

Austin still looked confused. "But I don't understand. How did he get so far into debt?"

"I don't know." She raised her gaze to his. "Sam joked about playing poker on occasion. I didn't think it was an obsession with him, but I assume now that it became one over time. It makes me wonder if Sam was looking for something different, something to make up for what we didn't have in our marriage. I don't think he was happy—at least, not happy being married to me."

"I find that hard to believe," Austin said. He spread his hands wide. "Sam never once said anything about not wanting to be married to you."

"Yet he envied your bachelor lifestyle," she felt compelled to point out.

He grimaced. "He may have mentioned that once or twice, although I didn't take him seriously. I know he cared for you Lindsey. I really think it might just have been the two of you getting married so young."

"Maybe." She tried to smile. "But caring isn't enough. Marriage is hard enough with people who are in love. Without love, it's almost unbearable. Especially when you add children to the mix."

He was silent for a moment. "You're right. Caring alone isn't enough."

She breathed a sigh of relief. He did understand after all. "Of course, I'm right." She strove for a casual tone. "So now that you understand where I'm coming from, there's no reason we can't be friends. Right?"

---

FRIENDS? Austin stared at her. He'd admired her from afar for years, had actually been jealous of Sam for having Lindsey as a wife, yet she wanted to be friends.

Sam, the jerk, had put her deeply in debt.

And then that same jerk had turned around and saved his life.

He ground his teeth together for a moment. Lindsey was right. Maybe Sam's heroic moment made up for the gambling. And he'd made his peace with God over the way Sam had saved his life. After all, it wasn't up to him to question God's plan.

But he hadn't asked Lindsey to marry him out of guilt. Or a sense of responsibility. And he definitely hadn't asked her to marry him because of a deathbed promise.

"Lindsey, do you know why I've never been in a serious relationship?"

She gave a careless shrug. "So many women, so little time?"

"Not funny." It was something his siblings would have said. He narrowed his gaze. "No. Because of you. Do you remember when you and I first met?"

She quirked a brow. "Oh, you mean when you brought that overdose patient in who threw up charcoal all over me?"

"Yeah." Maybe it wasn't glamorous but he remembered that day as if it were yesterday. Especially the keen disappointment when he'd caught sight of her wedding ring. He'd discovered later that she'd only been married for a couple of months then. If he'd met her first, before Sam, maybe things would have been different. For both of them. "You were wonderful to work with, not arrogant or snooty. Many of the other nurses acted as if they were better than us. Yes. that patient threw up all over you, but you weren't annoyed or disgusted. Instead, you are nothing but kind to the patient, nice to me and to the rest of the paramedic crew."

"It wasn't your fault or the patience fault that he threw up on me," she protested. "Charcoal is supposed to make you throw up. That's how you treat an overdose of sleeping pills."

"Very true, but I was so impressed with your kindness and compassion. The fact that you were totally hot was an added plus." He wasn't explaining himself very well. "There was just something about you that called to me in a way no other woman had done before. You have no idea how disappointed I was to discover you were married. I worked with Sam for several months before I met you, but I didn't realize you belonged to him until the day Sam invited me over for dinner."

Lindsey looked so surprised by his revelation that he had to smile. That night, when he'd come over for dinner, he'd been stunned to realize his secret crush was married to his partner. Holding a coherent conversation had been a challenge. It had been the first time in his life he'd ever been envious of any of his friends.

"From that day on," he added, "I remember thinking Sam was the luckiest guy in the world. And I told myself I needed to be happy for him. And I was. Truly."

"I never knew," she said in a low voice.

He snorted. "Of course not. I wouldn't make a move on my friend's wife. I tried to get over my infatuation with you by dating other women." He grimaced, remembering those first few dates had ended badly. "It didn't work. Every time I got to know one of them, I'd realize she couldn't compare to you. And when I went on out on a paramedic call and ended up with a patient that needed to be brought to the Sun Valley emergency department, I always looked for you. Just seeing you, even from afar, was enough to make me smile."

"I don't believe it," she whispered.

"Lindsey, I never allowed myself to fall in love with you, to even dream of having a chance with you, until Sam died. Yes, I promised him I'd take care of you and Josh. Why wouldn't I? There was nothing I wanted more than for the two of you to be safe and secure. It wasn't until I spent more time with you during the weeks after his death that I realized how I was falling in love with you."

Then they'd had their fight, when he tried to give her advice on raising her son. He remembered how she accused him of trying to run her life, and there had been a kernel of truth to that. Staying away from her had been the hardest thing he'd ever done.

Then God had brought her back into his life. A neighbor's fire had brought them together in the best way possible.

"I don't know what to say." Her gaze pleaded with him. "I'm shocked. All this time you never once hinted at any of this."

"If you don't feel the same way, that's fine." He forced himself to be diplomatic, refusing to pressure her. "But, Lindsey, every time we kiss, I get the impression that you feel something for me too."

"I did. I do." She covered her face with her hands. "I don't know."

He drew a deep breath. He could somewhat understand her confusion. After all this was a lot to comprehend at once. Impatience was his biggest fault. Yet he strove to find it now. "Don't throw away what we have—please? Give us a chance."

---

LINDSEY DIDN'T KNOW what to say or what to believe.

Austin claimed he loved her. Had always admired her. Had actually been jealous of Sam.

Ironic how Sam had wanted Austin's bachelor lifestyle while Austin had apparently longed for Sam's commitment.

Yet she had to believe he was telling the truth. His earnestness would have been impossible to fake. But what about her feelings?

She'd thought she'd been in love with Sam, but those feelings had changed. Looking back, she couldn't be certain she'd ever really loved him at all.

What if her feelings for Austin weren't what she thought, or worse, his feelings for her? What if they ended up drifting apart the way she and Sam had?

Just remembering his embrace, though, made her think this was different. She felt alive in Austin's arms. In a way she never had with Sam.

"Lindsey?" He was still waiting for an answer.

"I want to try again, Austin," she said slowly. "But you need to know, I'm scared."

"Scared?" He looked appalled. "Of me? I swear to you Lindsey, I would never do anything to hurt you or Josh. Never!"

She smiled. "Not of you, I'm afraid of ending up like my mother."

"Your mother?" He frowned. "I don't understand. I thought Sam told me your mother was dead."

"No. She just lives a lifestyle very different from mine. My dad walked out on us when I was at five. I don't remember him. Apparently he wasn't amount around much. Anyway, after he left my mother threw herself head-first into one bad relationship after another. Always for my benefit, of course, so that we could eat and have nice clothes to wear. And I would just get settled into one place when that relationship would end, and we'd move on to another."

"Wow, that must have been rough." He scowled. "Did any of these guys your mother stayed with mistreat you?"

"No, nothing like that," she hastened to reassure him. "It's just that, even at a young age, I could tell these guys were losers. I promised myself I'd never end up with a man like that. Sam was a handsome guy with a stable and impressive career as a paramedic and firefighter. He seemed to have his life together. In my eyes he was a hero. But in the end, when I discovered the extent of our financial debt, I realized he had been more like the guys my mother hooked up with than I'd ever imagined."

"Lindsey." He came around the table and reached for her hands. "You're an amazing emergency department nurse. You're wonderful with Josh. You are not your mother."

She had to admit he was right at least about her career. Her mother's lack of skilled training and steady employment had not helped their situation. They were often one step away from being kicked out of their apartment.

"I wish you could believe in me. In us. I know it's scary." His gaze searched hers. "Do you think I'm not a little afraid? My biggest fear is that I'll mess things up with you. I know marriage is a lifelong commitment. I want exactly what my parents have. And I think together we would. But you have to decide. All I can do is to promise to do whatever I can to make you happy."

She wanted to believe him. In her heart, she knew she didn't need Austin's help financially. Things might be tight, but she would get through it. But her feelings for him were impossible to ignore.

Could she do this? Could she trust her feelings and take the leap? Looking into Austin's deep green eyes, she began to believe she could. Her smile was tremulous. "I also want what your parents have. A marriage that is strong enough to last a lifetime."

He grinned, hope brightening his eyes. "Me, too. I love you Lindsey, and I promise to be a good husband and a father to Josh." His expression was gentle. "If you will give me a chance."

"I love you, Austin." Saying the words felt wonderful, especially when his eyes glittered with happiness. "I was afraid to admit it, but I realized a while ago how much I love you."

"I'm thrilled." He looked a bit dazed. "Because I love you, too."

"You should know Josh already loves you like a father. He's upset with me for moving us out of your house," she confided.

"Well, I can fix that." In a smooth move he swept her into his arms and carried her out the door of her tiny bungalow.

"I think you're carrying me over the wrong threshold," she said with a giggle.

He gently set her on her feet next to his car. "Lindsey, will you please marry me?"

Her smile widened. Maybe the third proposal was the

charm. "Yes, Austin. I will marry you."

"Thank You, God," he said in a heartfelt prayer. He gave her another one of his intense kisses. "We can build a new house if you like. Something completely ours—yours, mine and Josh's."

She shook her head. His offer was generous, but there was no need. Being in love with Austin felt right. He'd already loved her longer than Sam had. And he was the kind of guy who would always work toward a better marriage. He would talk things out. And he would listen to her concerns. The way he had just now.

"That's not necessary. Take me home, Austin."

"Are you sure?" He hesitated, giving her a chance to change her mind.

"I'm sure." She smiled. "We won't need a new house until after we're married and have filled your bedrooms with babies."

He flashed a sexy, hopeful grin. "Sounds like a perfect plan to me. And you should know, I plan on marrying you as soon as possible."

"I'd like that." She slid her arms around his waist. "As long as your family can be there to celebrate with us."

"Always," he murmured. "They love you almost as much as I do."

She rested her head on his chest, knowing that this time, she was making the right choice. His third marriage proposal had been the charm.


I HOPE you have enjoyed Austin and Lindsey's story in *Shattered Trust*. If you haven't given my new Oath of Honor series a try, you can check out the first book *Steele* by clicking here.

# DEAR READER

Thanks so much for reading my Monroe Family series. I'm truly blessed to have wonderful readers like you. I'm hard at work on my new Oath of Honor series. The first book, *Steele* is available now and *Brock* is available on my website.

Don't forget, you can purchase eBooks or audiobooks directly from my website will receive a 15% discount by using the code **LauraScott15**. I hope to have *Raelyn* up on my website by early March.

I adore hearing from my readers! I can be found through my website at https://www.laurascottbooks.com, via Facebook at https://www.facebook.com/LauraScott Books, Instagram at https://www.instagram.com/laurascott books/, and Twitter https://twitter.com/laurascottbooks. Please take a moment to subscribe to my YouTube channel at youtube.com/@LauraScottBooks-wr1xl?sub_confirmation=1. Also, take a moment to sign up for my monthly newsletter to learn about my new book releases! All subscribers receive a free novella not available for purchase on any platform.

Until next time,
Laura Scott